MONA OF THE MANOR

www.penguin.co.uk

Armistead Maupin

MONA OF THE MANOR

doubleday

TRANSWORLD PUBLISHERS
Penguin Random House, One Embassy Gardens,
8 Viaduct Gardens, London SW11 7BW
www.penguin.co.uk

Transworld is part of the Penguin Random House group of companies
whose addresses can be found at global.penguinrandomhouse.com

Penguin
Random House
UK

First published in Great Britain in 2024 by Doubleday
an imprint of Transworld Publishers

A CIP catalogue record for this book is available from the British Library.

ISBNs
9780857527073 hb
9780857527080 tpb

Printed and bound in Great Britain by Clays Ltd, Elcograf S.p.A.

The authorized representative in the EEA is Penguin Random House Ireland,
Morrison Chambers, 32 Nassau Street, Dublin D02 YH68.

Penguin Random House is committed to a sustainable future
for our business, our readers and our planet. This book is made
from Forest Stewardship Council® certified paper.

FOR CHRIS

FOREVER

As a woman, I have no country.
As a woman I want no country.
As a woman my country is the whole world.

—VIRGINIA WOOLF

1

THE MANOR AWAITS

According to her guidebook, they had already entered "the fabled heart of England," but Rhonda Blaylock could see only a watery green blur from the window of the train as it rumbled through the countryside. The rain hadn't let up since they'd left London.

"We'll be nice and cozy at the manor house," she said, keeping things light with her husband, who was already being grumpy about the weather. She loved hearing the words *manor house* trip so naturally off her tongue. She had never before even had occasion to say that, unless you counted Manor House Barbecue, where she and Ernie celebrated their silver anniversary back home in North Carolina. Now they were headed for a real manor house—one built in Elizabethan times—and she could barely contain her excitement.

"Did you tell them when we're coming?" muttered Ernie, his face pressed sullenly against the window.

"Of course." She had called from the station in Oxford for

just that reason. "A nice-sounding man said he'd heat up our bed pans."

Her husband turned and gaped at her. "Do *what*?"

She giggled at her mistake. "Bedwarmers . . . whatever. It's something old-timey they do for guests when they turn down your bed. I think he was the butler."

"Why?"

"He called himself Wilfred. No last name."

"I thought butlers were always addressed by their last name."

Now Ernie was just looking for a fight, and she would have none of that. This would not be the costliest accommodation on their ten-city European tour (that title went to a fancy Marriott in Paris), but it was the one that Rhonda had dreamed of ever since she'd received a postcard confirming receipt of their Diners Club payment. On one side there was a quaint pen-and-ink drawing of Easley House; on the other was a personal message from the lady of the manor. "Welcome to my home," it said, and it was signed (in purple ink, no less) by Lady Roughton herself. "We're so looking forward to your visit."

That sounded sweetly personal to Rhonda. Not just looking forward but *so* looking forward, like an old friend from high school welcoming you to her beach cottage in Nags Head. But this was an English aristocrat, a total stranger really, whose family had lived in this house for almost five centuries. Such easy graciousness seemed above and beyond, even if it was costing the Blaylocks a thousand pounds for a three-night stay.

She was so glad she'd come across that little classified ad in *Southern Living* magazine. This was going to be something special.

They got off the train, as instructed, at Moreton-in-Marsh, a quaint village built of golden Cotswold limestone. The wind and driving rain played havoc with their collapsible umbrellas and sent Ernie into another tirade.

"We'll get you a nice hot toddy at the Black Bear," she said. hooking her arm into Ernie's as they scrambled up the street, wheeling their luggage behind them. Wilfred had told her about the pub and how to ask the bartender for a driver to Easley House.

So that's what they did when they got inside and shook off the rain.

"The driver's name is Colin," said the bartender. "Be here in twenty minutes. Bald fellow with big black eyebrows. Two hot toddies coming up. How 'bout some lovely Scotch eggs on the house while you're waiting?"

"What's that?" Ernie asked suspiciously.

Rhonda told him before the bartender could. "It's a hard-boiled egg wrapped in sausage and fried in breadcrumbs. C'mon, Ernie, you like all those things." She had just read about Scotch eggs in an English romance novel, so it tickled her to be offered one in real life. "We'll take two," she told the bartender. "And never mind that face my husband is making. He's been working too hard lately."

Ernie had put his law practice on hold for the better part of a year so he could run the Jesse Helms Reelection Campaign in Eastern North Carolina. The experience had exhausted him, leaving him more ill-tempered than usual. The senator had won, of course (he always did), but he never sent so much as a thank-you note to Ernie after the election, much less a hoped-for invitation to lunch with Jesse in the Senate cafeteria. Since then, for some reason, Rhonda had watched her husband grow increasingly irritable with people in service positions—whether it be their faithful maid, Alva, or this nice bartender, or the waiter in London at Simpson's in the Strand, who didn't carve the roast beef the way Ernie liked.

The bartender gave them a crooked smile as he set the eggs down in front of them. "So you're friends of Lady Roughton's?"

"No," she replied. She was thrilled to be mistaken for a friend of Lady Roughton and wondered briefly if her Montaldo's raincoat and Hermès fox-hunting scarf had created that impression. She had to ask: "Why did you think we were friends?"

The bartender just shrugged as he wiped the bar. "You're Americans, aren't you?"

Ernie's eyes narrowed. "Yes. Proud ones."

Rhonda scolded her husband with a glance before turning back to the bartender. "Does Lady Roughton know a lot of Americans?"

Another shrug. "She's American. I imagine she does."

"She's *American*? I thought the family dated back to Elizabethan times."

"It does. But she came along about ten years ago when she married Lord Teddy. Then the poor sod died and left her to run the place. Seems to enjoy it, though. Told me it's her destiny to run a house. Said it ran in the family. Don't know what she meant by that . . . but."

"You know her, then?"

"Everybody knows her. She comes into the village to shop. So you're just . . . paying guests?"

Rhonda murmured in the affirmative, feeling somehow shamed.

Their driver, the bald and bushy-browed Colin, was a man of few words. On the twenty-minute drive from the pub to Easley House he barely spoke at all, even when Rhonda made appreciative comments about the scenery: the rolling meadows, a wayside chapel with its windows glowing pink in the rain, an ancient wooden barn, ramshackle but somehow quite beautiful. Every cottage she saw along the way was made of the same golden limestone she had seen in the village. That uniformity made everything seem related, scattered offspring of the great house itself, which suddenly leapt into view as they rounded a sunken lane.

Rhonda gasped as she saw it. "Oh Ernie, look!"

"I see it," said her husband.

Easley House was a rambling two-story structure with deep gables cut into a steep roof. The limestone here had darkened with weather and age to a variegated orangey-gray, like the hide of a tiger. There were wedding cake crenelations along the top and a front door so imposing you could see it from a great distance. Smoke curled from a gargantuan chimney as Colin pulled into a rutted driveway at the side of the house. The overall effect was one of storybook dilapidation. Rhonda felt her heart race as she imagined their entrance to this place.

"How do we get to the front door?" she asked as Ernie unloaded their luggage.

"They don't use the front door."

"He means guests don't," said Ernie.

"No sir. No one does. It's nailed shut. Lady Mo says it's a hassle."

"Who?"

"Lady Roughton's name is Mona, Some of us call her Lady Mo."

"Well, isn't that cute? Like Lady Di. Do you think she would mind if we called . . . ?"

"What do we owe you?" asked Ernie, obviously impatient with the chitchat.

"Ten quid even," said the driver.

Ernie fished a bill from his wallet and handed it to the driver.

"Thank you, Colin. How the hell do we get in?"

"Right there, sir." He indicated a nondescript door in front of the car. "Just follow that hallway until you reach the great hall. Someone will collect you."

So she and Ernie, tugging their luggage, rattled down a moldy passageway lined with garden tools and rusty bicycles.

Ernie grunted audibly. "A thousand pounds," he muttered.

"Shhhhh," she commanded, pressing her finger to her lips. She could already sense that the hallway was about to end, and she didn't want her Ladyship hearing their graceless entrance. Sure enough, the muddy hoes and rakes gave way to a dark-green wall filled with sullen ancestral portraits and murky landscapes and a tattered poster of a stained-glass window with the word *Erasure* at the top, which she assumed was religious in nature.

Then suddenly they were there in the great hall, a vaulting space with firelight flickering on the walls. The fireplace was enormous, high enough to stand in, she reckoned, as she grabbed

Ernie's hand for a moment of awestruck appreciation. Lemony light from a huge stained-glass window created the illusion of sunshine on their faces.

"What's that noise?" Ernie asked suspiciously.

She could hear it, too. An intermittent pinging sound that seemed to surround them.

It was Ernie, naturally, who figured it out. "The goddamn roof is leaking." He pointed triumphantly to a saucepan on the floor as if he'd just uncovered a clue to an unsolved murder. It was already half filled with rain, and there were three or four others around the room, strategically placed to collect drips.

There was no one in sight to greet them. Not even a desk with a bell to ring.

"Helloo," she called, trying to sound as pleasant as possible. "Company's coming." It instantly sounded foolish to her ears, but it was all she could think to say.

Ernie rolled his eyes with a labored sigh. She knew he was about to blow his top again, but he didn't get the chance, thank goodness. A young man had rushed out of a swinging door with a tray full of tea things. He was sporting a plaid bow tie and a sleeveless argyle sweater with a noticeable hole in it. He had soft Afro-styled hair and a cafe au lait complexion that she would have described as mulatto before Oprah made it clear that they don't like that.

He greeted Rhonda with a look of sweet mortification. He was in his midtwenties, she supposed, but his embarrassment made him seem younger. "You must be Mrs. Blaylock." He set the tray down on a dark oak sideboard. "This was supposed to be your welcome tea. So sorry, got me signals crossed. Colin usually honks when he leaves. Shall I set up in your room or . . . pour you a cuppa right here?"

She was touched by his flustered effort at setting things right.

"Why, I think we'd like a cup of tea right here," she said. This is Mr. Blaylock . . . we're both chilled to the bone. This was not at all how she expected a butler to look, but she recognized his voice from the phone. "You must be Wilfred."

"Guilty as charged," he said, setting up some delicate mismatched cups and saucers. His hand was shaking visibly as he tried to pour the tea. Then he lost his grip and dropped the tarnished silver teapot directly onto one of the cups, shattering it. "Bollocks!" he muttered, before looking at Rhonda with a look of sheepish contrition. "Pardon me Anglo-Saxon."

"We don't need tea," Ernie said gruffly. "Just show us to our room, please."

Rhonda felt awful for the young man, who was just trying to do his job, after all. "It was a lovely gesture," she told him as he hastily collected fragments of china before picking up their luggage. "Lady Roughton will be down shortly to greet you," he said. "Your room is up those stairs, third door on the left. I'll put your bags there."

And with that he was gone, leaving the Blaylocks alone in the great hall again.

"A thousand pounds," grumbled Ernie.

"Just shut up," said Rhonda under her breath.

"Are you telling your husband to shut up?"

"Yes, Ernie, I believe I am."

"Well. I'm telling you that we should have had the goddamn

sense to stay two more days at the Dorchester, but no . . . you had to a have your la-di-da country house . . ."

He cut himself off when they heard footsteps on the stairs.

The woman who came into view had ringlets of red hair spilling down her head like lava. She was wearing riding breeches and a moss-green velvet off-the-shoulder top. She looked to be somewhere in her late forties. "Welcome to my little bordello," she said as she strode noisily down the stairs. "I'm Mona Roughton. Sorry about the drippy-drips. They come every year no matter how much we patch the roof. I hope my son poured you a nice cup of tea."

Her son? This pale-skinned white woman? Rhonda struggled for words. "Oh . . . well . . . yes . . . Wilfred, you mean. He was very nice . . . very considerate." She shot a quick look at Ernie to make sure he wasn't about to mention the shattered teacup lying in full view on the abandoned tray. She didn't want to cause trouble for Wilfred.

"We're a family operation," said Lady Roughton, as if reading Rhonda's mind. "You won't find a lot of staff around here unless you count our gardener, Mr. Hargis, who knows how the old girl runs . . . or doesn't run, as the case may be." She extended her hand to Rhonda. "I take it you're the Blaylocks. If you're not . . . get your ass out of my ancestral home."

She knew this was meant to be friendly, so she managed a chuckle. Ernie, for the moment at least, seemed stunned into silence.

"C'mon," said Lady Roughton, beckoning them to the stairs. "You'll want a good soak and a nap, won't you? Your room has the best clawfoot tub in the house and some fabulous lavender bath salts. I'll show you around before dinner, but you're free to poke around on your own. There's no one else in the house at the moment, and nothing's off-limits. Consider this your own private Disneyland. That's what I do every single day."

So they followed her up the stairs to a large, high-ceilinged room with a threadbare oriental carpet and a canopied four-poster bed. There was an en suite bathroom off to one side that seemed to have recently been painted a lurid shade of purple. Ernie, who'd been skulking about the room in silence, felt compelled to examine the label on a sleek glass bottle by the bedside. "'Malvern Water,'" he read.

"The best there is," said Lady Roughton, "The queen travels the world with it. Tastes a *whole* lot better than what comes out of these old pipes. That shit's Jacobean at the very least. She moved to the window and flung open a damask curtain that must have been red at some point in its long life. "You have a stunning view of our folly. See? Up there?"

Rhonda joined her at the window. Before her lay a steep green hillside with a little dunce-capped pavilion at the top. Lady Roughton explained: "My late husband's ancestor, the umpteenth Earl of Who-the-fuck-knows-what, built it to escape from his wife, who was deeply religious, if you know what I mean."

Rhonda did not know what she meant, so she welcomed the distraction of a big yellow dog that had just loped into the room to nuzzle her leg.

"Well, who's this sweet thing?"

"That's Miss Vanilla Wafer, but you may call her Nilla. She has the run of the house. If she drops something dead in your room it just means she likes you."

Ernie, who often preferred dogs to people, came over to squat and scratch the dog behind her ear. "You're very good girl, aren't you? Aren't you, Nilla?" Rhonda liked seeing these rare displays of tenderness from her husband. It made him seem more human to outsiders. He looked up at Lady Roughton. "She's a beauty, all right. Do you hunt with her?"

The lady of the manor looked aghast. "You mean go out and *shoot things?*"

"Sure. It's what they're bred for. See that big soft jaw? He jostled the dog's mouth. "It's there so they can retrieve dead pheasant without mangling them."

"Well . . . nice to know, but we don't do that at Easley. Not on my watch anyway. No blood sports around here. Nilla has to make do with voles."

There was tension in the air, so Rhonda tried to change the subject. "I'm afraid I don't know what a vole is."

"Just a sort of field mouse," said Lady Roughton, heading for the door with the dog. "Time for me to bake bread. Dinner's at eight in the great hall. If you hear barking, pay no heed. Nilla gets excited when she smells bread rising. She's such a big ol' lesbian, that one."

And with that she charged off.

Ernie turned to his wife. "We're getting out of here," he said.

"I'm running a tub," said Rhonda.

2

E AT THE FRIDGE

Wilfred was in the kitchen, presiding over a steaming cauldron of lamb stew, when Mona burst through the swinging door.

"That smells divoon," she said.

"Well . . . it's me specialty, innit."

Lamb stew was one of Wilfred's three "specialties," the others being cottage pie and battered haddock, but three was generally all they needed when it came to feeding guests. Most guests never stayed for longer than three nights once the novelty wore off and the damp set in. Once they realized there was one crappy little black-and-white TV in the whole joint and old Mr. Hargis with his lazy eye had a way of turning up when they least expected him. Easley House offered character over convenience. Some people got that: others, fuck 'em.

She asked Wilfred what he thought of the Blaylocks.

He shrugged, still stirring the stew. "Nice enough, I guess."

"And tea service went well?"

Another shrug.

"You're hungover, aren't you?"

He stopped stirring and looked at her. "And why do you say that, your Ladyship?" He never used that term unless he was being snide.

"Well," she replied, "it's Monday, and you went into London this weekend, and you're always a clumsy mess after you've done E at the Fridge . . . and there are incriminating shards of teacup out there with your fingerprints all over them. Will that do?"

A smile crept over his face. "Very good, Miss Marple."

"Did you meet anybody nice?"

"Mmm."

"He's not upstairs, I hope?"

Wilfred shook his head. "He saw me off at the train station after breakfast."

Wilfred's last pickup had stayed overnight at Easley House, unbeknownst to anyone but Wilfred, so Mona had woken at dawn to a blood-curdling scream when a paying guest from Derbyshire—a retired librarian, no less—had crossed paths with a butt-naked Egyptian bodybuilder wandering the hallway in search of a loo. It had not been pretty.

"All I want is a little warning," she said. "That poor woman was traumatized." She hesitated a moment. "You're being careful, aren't you?"

"I promise you, Mo . . . there's no one upstairs."

"I didn't mean that. I meant about . . . you know, safe sex. E can make you feel invincible. If you get carried away in the moment, you'll forget all about—"

"For God's sake, Mo! We just wanked each other off in the alley."

Mona blinked at him. "And he still put you on the train in the morning?"

"Yes!"

"That's the sweetest thing I've ever heard."

Wilfred shrugged. "He liked me. Go figure."

"You're welcome to bring him home some time . . . and anyone else, for that matter."

She was trying not to come off like a controlling mother, even though, technically, that's what she was. Wilfred had lived at Easley for a decade, but she'd been forced to adopt him five years earlier when he was still underage and Thatcher's immigration goons had come sniffing around with threats of deportation to Australia. That was ridiculous, of course, since Wilfred had been born in a squat in Brixton, but their intentions had been obvious: they didn't want an undocumented Anglo Aborigine running around free in a stately home. So Mona had documented him. When he officially became her son, she gave him one of the dramatic rooms under the eaves.

"That room is obviously made for lurvvve," she said, drawing out the word like Barry White to show she was cool about overnight guests. Wilfred had festooned the room with rugs and bedspreads he found in the attic, which, along with some candles and pillows and hanging incense burners, gave it the raffish air of a seraglio. And this, she had realized with a twinge of nostalgia, was exactly the sort of lair she would have created for herself back in the day in San Francisco (discounting, of course, the ubiquitous pinups of Wilfred's idol, George Michael).

She wanted Wilfred to find someone, she really did, but she shuddered at the thought of him cruising London blissed out on Ecstasy now that the plague was raging worse than ever. She had hoped he might meet someone nice in town—town being their pissant little village of Easley-on-Hill, where Wilfred sometimes cruised church fetes and football matches in hopes of meeting someone gay who actually lived in the county. His one good prospect, a blond and bubbly vicar's son he had taken home one Christmas, had dubious motives. As Wilfred had put it at the time: "He just wanted to get into me house, not me knickers." Easley House held abiding appeal for some social-climbing locals, even if the hereditary line had died out with Teddy. There was magic still to be found in these crumbling umber stones, and no one knew that better than Mona, who made a living off the curiosity of strangers. She had loved the thought of sharing that magic with this sweet kid.

He was just sixteen when he moved in, a veritable foundling left on her doorstep by her friend Michael Tolliver when he crashed the house looking for her. Wilfred had been smitten with Michael at the time, but Michael, honorably, had refused his advances. When Michael returned to San Francisco after a few weeks, Wilfred had remained at Easley and in no time at all became a member Mona's "logical family," a term her father/mother was fond of using. After all these years, without ever asking for one, Mona had a son.

There was talk in the village, of course, that she and Wilfred were doing it. She saw the smirks exchanged when the two of them went in for weekly staples, and it bugged the shit out of her, since it implied cradle robbing on her part, if not flat-out pedophilia. It was an open secret in Gloucestershire that her late husband had been a raging queen, so how dare they suspect her of such low-rent heterosexuality? *There's nothing to see here,* she wanted to yell at the smirkers. *Just a couple of queers making a family!*

The cradle-robbing gossip died a quick death when Mona struck up an affair with Poppy Gallagher, the ravishing postmistress of Chipping Campden. Poppy had handled Mona's growing volume of mail from prospective lodgers. "I'm giving you your own box," she had confided one day from beneath a slab of sleek chestnut hair, and it was abundantly clear what else she was offering. They were on each other that afternoon and had gone hot and heavy all summer, sometimes at Easley, sometimes at Poppy's converted water mill in Blockley, but their ardor had cooled by the first frost. They still got together, but nowadays they were more likely to swap garden cuttings than cunnilingus. She and Poppy were occasional fuck buddies with domestic benefits, and that was not a bad thing to be in Mona's estimation.

The truth was she *liked* being single at Easley House. There were always Wilfred and the guests whenever she craved company, and she loved the sweet, embracing solitude of this place, the empty rooms and tangled gardens just waiting to enfold her whenever she needed peace. Sometimes she felt that this house had been waiting for her all her life.

Or she had been waiting for it.

The downpour had grown more fierce, slashing against the diamond-shaped panes above the kitchen sink, so Mona and Wilfred went into the great hall to check on the state of the drip pans. One of them, as she had suspected, was on the verge of overflowing.

"I think we should move the table," she said, "just to be safe. If the roof leaks on that woman's careful hair, there's gonna be hell to pay. And we're gonna need more logs for the fire, don't you think? It's colder than a witch's titty in here."

Wilfred agreed on all points and tried to help with the table, an oaken monstrosity that impressed guests with its baronial pretensions but was an absolute motherfucker to lift. "Should I get Mr. Hargis?" asked Wilfred, when their efforts proved futile.

"Only if you want to watch him have a stroke." She stood up and rotated her torso to make sure she hadn't thrown out her back. "If the leak moves, we'll put a drip pan on the table and move Mrs. Blaylock. It'll be picturesque. They'll talk about it for years back in Alabama."

"North Carolina," said Wilfred.

"Same difference," said Mona.

Wilfred pondered something for a moment. "Do you think they're racist?"

Mona shrugged. "Not so far. Did you pick up on something?"

"Nope. They seemed okay to me."

"Well, we can't afford to split hairs, can we? The less we know about the politics of our guests the better. We're just here to take their money and show 'em a good time."

Wilfred was grinning at her. "As your gran used to say."

Of all the louche particulars of Mona's grab bag of a life, the one that impressed Wilfred the most was the fact that her late grandmother had run a brothel in Nevada. He brought it up at the slightest provocation. She smiled to acknowledge the obvious parallels between her life and the life of that other Mona, her namesake. "Well, we do need the cash, that's for damn sure. The Blaylocks just paid for our water heater, and not a moment too soon."

That's how she'd come to think of her paying guests: necessities who paid for necessities. The honeymooning couple from Milton Keynes had covered repairs to Teddy's old Toyota. Some hearty Texas dykes had provided groceries for a month and a new shipment of Malvern Water. That history professor from Glasgow had bailed her out with the power company just as she was on the verge of having to pretend that candlelight was their preferred form of illumination. They were pushed to the limits sometimes, but somehow, in spite of everything, the house always came through for them.

Mr. Hargis arrived in the great hall staggering under a mammoth bucket of daffodils still dripping with rain. "I thought you might like to bring a little spring indoors, milady." Early on, Mona had tried to get the old codger to knock off the milady shit, but had given up the effort after she realized how much it meant to him. For better or worse, she *was* his Lady, just as Teddy had been his Lord for fifty years, and it wasn't right to take that away from him in his dotage.

"You're my hero," she said, receiving the flowers and stuffing them into a big copper pot on the table. This would be proof of the season, she figured, harbingers of the famous English spring the Blaylocks had paid big bucks for. "Bring us some water for the daffies, would you, sweetheart?"

Wilfred widened his eyes. "You could always put them under a drip."

"Very funny. Now get a move on. They're gonna be coming down those stairs after their nap, and we've got a show to do."

She slapped him on his denim butt to show that she wasn't mad.

When Wilfred was gone, Mr. Hargis helped her stuff daffodils into pots. They were silent until the old man uttered a tentative "Milady?"

"What, Mr. Hargis?" She probably sounded a little short when she said this, but she was pretty sure she knew what was coming next. These days the old man rarely returned from his garden without a significant sighting of some sort.

"The Old Gypsy is back," he said.

"Oh yeah?" she said noncommittally.

"Yes, milady. Up by the folly this time."

"Did he . . . do you think he slept there?"

"Couldn't tell. He was gone in a flash."

Mona thrust a daffodil into a Mason jar. "You know I don't mind, don't you?"

"Don't mind what, milady?"

"If Gypsies come onto the estate."

"It's for your protection, milady,"

"I know, and I appreciate that, but Gypsies are just other people who live in this county." There was, in fact, a vividly painted wagon that sometimes parked in the village green, where a dour woman in a shawl sat with her sloe-eyed children, waiting to charge wide-eyed weekenders for photographs. "They're part of the landscape," she added, "nothing to fret about."

The gardener gaped at her. "They steal babies, milady."

"Well, we're in luck then," said Mona, smiling, "because we're fresh out of babies at the moment. Unless you count Wilfred, and he's big enough to defend himself."

Poor Mr. Hargis looked crushed under the weight of her smartass tone.

"You know that's an old wives' tale," she added more gently.

"I just don't trust that shifty old Roma. Always skulking about. I chased him out of the barn last week. You know how he is."

As a matter of fact, Mona did *not* know how he was. In all her rambles about the estate over the past decade she had never once seen this intruder. He was Mr. Hargis's own private boogeyman, someone who seemed less and less likely to be real as the years wore on. She never challenged his existence, however, because she figured this was the old gardener's way of being their protector, their ever-vigilant eye on Easley. In every version of this story, whether up at the folly or in the woods or over at the barn, he invariably chased the Old Gypsy away.

Mona set the table for the Blaylocks, laying out her Wedgwood amid tarnished pewter candlesticks and daffodils in Mason jars. She was especially pleased with the hand-painted place markers that Poppy Gallagher had personalized for these guests. EASLEY HOUSE WELCOMES THE BLAYLOCKS was the inscription, and the words were intertwined with Victorian violets and rosebuds. At no charge to Mona, Poppy had created similar mementos for half a dozen other guests, and they had proven a hit. The secret to hospitality, Mona realized, lay not in extravagance but in small inexpensive details that make guests feel important. Her guests invariably took those place markers home with them to Des Moines or Milton Keynes.

"I hope I'm not too late for the tour!"

Mona looked up to see Mrs. Blaylock on the staircase, obviously dressed for dinner in a pink-and-green skirt-and-blouse combo that Mona's biological mother might have worn to a realtor's convention in Minneapolis.

"Well, somebody looks nice," said Mona.

Her guest did a shy little dip that could easily have been mistaken for a curtsey. "Drip-dry for travel, I'm afraid. I hope it's appropriate for this house."

Mona snorted. "Everything's appropriate for this house." Almost on cue, Nilla started barking in the kitchen. "What did I tell you?" said Mona. "She's barking because the bread's ready. Hang on a sec, would you?" She rushed out, snatched the bread from the oven, placed it on an upper shelf, and returned to Mrs. Blaylock: "Now then . . . the tour."

"If it's too much trouble right now—"

"Stop that. You apologize too much."

That brought a nervous titter. "Do I?"

"Yes, and I'll have none of that, Mrs. Blaylock." She chuckled inwardly at the pompous sound of that. "Is there a first name I can use with you?"

The woman was already blushing. "Of course. It's Rhonda."

"Really? Like Rhonda Fleming?"

"Yes! That's where my mother got the name."

Mona lifted her hands in celebration of this unexpected mutuality. "My mother was *always* going on about Rhonda Fleming, because she was a famous redhead, and my mother didn't want me feeling bad about . . . this." She thrust her hand into her springy red curls.

"But your hair is so pretty," said Rhonda. "Anyone would want that."

Mona shrugged. "Not my mother, apparently."

"Well, I'll bet your husband loved it."

"Actually," said Mona, feeling reckless around this demure Carolina housewife, "I was dyeing it blonde at the time. Something to do with Lady Di, I suppose."

"Oh . . . you know her?"

"No . . . but my husband did. Slightly. He went to a few soirees where she was present. I thought he might go for the look. He didn't. I sure as hell didn't either."

Rhonda smiled feebly. "The things we do for our men."

Indeed, thought Mona. "Will your husband be joining us for the tour?"

"Uh . . . no, actually . . . he found a Tom Clancy book in the room, and he's just devouring it."

Mona smiled at her. "You know, someone left that behind, so I keep it there for the men. They love all the war shit, don't they? C'mon, Rhonda! There are wonders to behold."

And with that she led the way up the stairs.

The tour had evolved over time into a veritable potpourri of poppycock. Teddy's father, who had been lord of the manor after the war, had created brass nameplates for the family portraits, so that was a realistic starting point from which Mona's fancy could take flight. Previous spiels had gone like this: "And here is the beautiful Lady Daphne Roughton, who died very young in 1647, when she flung herself from a church tower in Spain. She did it at the very moment her lover, a Castilian prince, was inside the church being married to another woman."

The story was always a crowd-pleaser and could be modified to keep things fresh for Mona. Sometimes the church was a cathedral in France. Sometimes, if Mona was feeling benevolent, there was no suicide at all, and Lady Daphne would die of heart failure in the arms of a handsome stable boy—or a pretty chambermaid—depending on the tastes of the guests. These old faces on the walls were the sourdough starter for the fresh bread of her imagination, and that, she would argue with no shame whatsoever, was her greatest gift to her guests.

Today, on a whim, she had something different in store for Mrs. Blaylock.

"Well, that's just the saddest thing," said Rhonda, stepping back to study the delicate pink features of the doomed Lady Daphne. "Imagine being charged by a cow!"

"I know," said Mona in a hushed tone. "Awful."

"I thought only bulls charged people."

"No, no. Cows can be quite aggressive." Rhonda, who could very well have been raised on a farm, did not look entirely convinced, so Mona improvised: "And she was . . . you know, pregnant at the time and miscarried and lost a lot of blood." She hung her head in a shameless imitation of mourning. "And that little boy was supposed to be lord of the manor."

Rhonda's brow wrinkled. "So they already knew it was a boy? Could they do that in those days?"

This was beginning to feel uncomfortably like a cross-examination, so Mona made a hasty escape into the truth. "By the way, see those scallop shells up there?" She pointed to the ornamentation along the colonnade. "Do you know what that represents?"

"Someone liked the sea? Or missed it maybe?"

Mona smiled. "Good answer, but no. The scallop shell was an ancient vaginal symbol. She fanned her palms out in front of her crotch to demonstrate the concept. "*Comme ça*. Isn't that fascinating? They're all over this house. It's the female version of a phallic symbol. My husband told me that the first time I came here, and it completely endeared me to him."

Rhonda was blushing again. "I'm so sorry about your loss."

It took Mona a moment. "Oh, my husband, you mean. How do you know about that?"

"Uh . . . the bartender at the Black Bear."

"Of course. How does anyone know about anything?"

Rhonda looked mortified. "I hope I wasn't out of turn to—"

"No, no. It's common knowledge. He died about five years ago. Cancer."

That was the truth, of course, but only part of it.

"That must've been hard for you," said Rhonda. "I'm so sorry."

Sympathy for her widowhood was one of the few things that still embarrassed Mona, since she knew how little she deserved it. In fact, on some dark nights of the soul, lying abed at Easley, she went so far as to blame herself for his death.

"Death is never easy," she said, hoping that would put an end to things.

It did not.

"If you don't mind my asking," said Rhonda, "how did you two meet?"

"It was sort of a whirlwind thing," said Mona, resorting to her standard answer. "I was living in Seattle at the time, and we corresponded for a while, and eventually . . . he sent for me. We were married in that little chapel you passed on the way in."

Rhonda actually clutched her heart. "He sent for you! What a lovely way to put it. He sent for you!"

Yeah, thought Mona, and it sounds a helluva lot better than "mail-order bride."

3

THE MINSTRELS' GALLERY

Wilfred had never known a childhood in which he could claim some space as his own, so he was catching up at Easley. He loved living in a house so large that there was always somewhere new to get lost, some secret cubbyhole that invited his colonization. You could sometimes find him curled up in the window seat in the great hall, where a teenager named Lucinda had scratched graffiti into the bubbly yellow glass in 1723. Or in the attic, where the dark ribs of the roof beams made him feel like Jonah in the belly of the whale. Or in the folly on the hill, where he kept an aluminum folding chair and a tin of hash for jolly summer afternoons.

His favorite hideaway, by far, was the minstrels' gallery above the great hall, where musicians had once played for the guests down below. Now it was just one more place to store stuff, so it was crammed with old mattresses and broken furniture that was too historic to throw away. Wilfred had taken one of those mattresses and pulled it out to the very edge of the gallery, where he could lie down behind a waist-high curtain and listen to the chatter of the dining guests. He loved hovering above them like an eavesdropping kestrel.

He had gone to the gallery tonight to get an honest verdict on his lamb stew. When Mo brought it out with the roasted vegetables and lifted the lid of their fancy Italian casserole dish there were murmurs of appreciation from both the Blaylocks, but he knew not to trust that until Mo had returned to the kitchen. People always made a fuss when she was around.

"This really is so scrumptious," said Mrs. Blaylock after they'd eaten alone for a while. "A real home-cooked English meal."

"Mmm," said her husband, apparently in agreement.

"I'm sure it's much better than what we would have gotten at the Dorchester . . . or, for that matter, the Senate cafeteria."

"Just leave it alone, Rhonda!"

"All right . . . but that's what you should do. Put it behind you. Forgive me, Ernie, but . . . I just don't think he's a nice man."

"He's a great American patriot!"

"That may be, but . . . he doesn't treat people kindly."

"You don't know what you're talking about!"

"I know how he treated you. And I know how he speaks about those poor people who can't help themselves."

"What poor people?"

"You know. The ones who are dying.

"*Are you comparing me to a bunch of goddamn perverts?*"

There was a crash that sounded like their fancy Italian casserole shattering on the floor.

Then Mrs. Blaylock said in a lower, more urgent tone: "For God's sake, Ernie. We're in someone's house. You're going to have to control your—"

"Don't tell me what I have to do. If you give me lip one more time, so help me . . ."

He didn't finish because Mo had entered the hall.

"Have we had a little whoopsie?" She was obviously trying to sound chipper.

"I'm afraid so," said Mrs. Blaylock. "I was serving my husband some stew, and . . ."

"No sweat, Rhonda. Just leave it where it lays. There's plenty more stew in the kitchen."

"Ernie, would you like some more—?"

"No," her husband said. "I think it's time for us to hit the sack."

"There's a lovely pudding," Mo offered feebly.

"I think we're done," said Rhonda. "I hope you don't mind."

"Of course not," said Mo.

There was the sound of chairs scraping the floor as the Blaylocks got up.

Wilfred crept out of the gallery and hurried down to the kitchen, where he found Mo already throwing shards of pottery into the rubbish bin. She looked up at him with weary resignation. "There's a lot of clumsiness with crockery in this house today."

"That wasn't clumsiness," said Wilfred.

"What?"

"They had a fight. I think he threw that at her."

"What? How could you possibly know . . . ?" She didn't finish, because she knew the answer already. "Have you been lurking in the minstrels' gallery again?"

Wilfred shrugged a silent yes.

"That's so creepy, Wilfred."

"Not as creepy as that bloke."

"C'mon. He threw that big heavy casserole at her?"

"I've seen worse," said Wilfred. "Me dad threw a toolbox at me."

"Well, your dad was a certified prick."

"How do you know this one isn't?"

Mo thought for a moment. "He seems a little moody, sure, but . . . What were they fighting about?"

"Hard to tell. Somebody they both know who she doesn't think is a nice person. And he yelled something about perverts before the casserole hit the floor."

"*Perverts?*"

"Yeah. He said she was comparing him to perverts."

Mo went to the sink and washed her hands ferociously, drying them on a tea towel. "This is a perfect example of why we shouldn't be spying on our guests. We don't need to know these things, Wilfred, and we can't afford to be refunding another credit card. We cannot have another Mr. Gay Cairo!"

That was Mona's cute name for his naked Egyptian trick.

"That's not bloody fair, Mo! I'm doing me best. I just went up there to see what they thought of me stew. I can't help it if—"

"You can help not spying, goddamnit. You're going to ruin us, Wilfred, if you keep up like this. No one will ever come here again, and we'll be flat broke, and we'll have no choice but to sell Easley to Fabia Dane."

Mo was always threatening to sell Easley to Fabia Dane, a toffee-nosed Tory bitch whose husband had made a fortune off Dane Vinegar Crisps. Fabia had always wanted to be the mistress of Easley, but Mo had rebuffed her offers as long as Wilfred could remember. She wouldn't even buy the crisps when they went into the pub.

"That will never happen," he said with a crooked grin.

"Don't be so sure." She gazed at him sternly before a sudden tenderness overtook her and she cupped her hand against his cheek. "Just be more careful, sweetness."

"Do you want me to take the bed warmer to their room?"

Mo mulled that over. "No," she said. "Let's leave them alone tonight. Things were looking pretty tense there."

Wilfred was relieved. "You noticed it, then?"

"Well . . . I don't think he threw that casserole at her, if that's what you mean."

Wilfred did the dishes then put the leftover stew and the untouched trifle into the fridge. He hurried up to his room afterward, realizing there was still time to catch *Ab Fab* on the telly. When he passed the Blaylocks' room, he noticed light coming under the door, so he stopped for a moment and listened. No one was talking, but there was the faint sound of—what? whimpering? It was a pitiful sound like a wounded animal.

He moved closer to listen.

The door swung open, making him jump back. Mr. Blaylock stood there, glowering at him in a nightshirt. "Something I can help you with, son?"

"No . . . I . . . so sorry to disturb. I promised Mrs. Blaylock a bed warmer."

"We don't need that. We're in bed already."

Wilfred backed away. "Righty ho."

He scurried down the hallway to his room. Something was

seriously wrong here, but he knew not to tell Mo about it. She would only accuse him of snooping again.

He flopped on his bed and turned on the telly. Patsy and Edina helped to lighten his spirits when they shared a bottle of vodka that Patsy had hidden under the bathroom sink.

When *Ab Fab* was over he abandoned the telly and turned to his other source of comfort: a box of letters he'd received from his friend Michael over the past decade. There were thirty-two of them in all. Michael had proposed they become pen pals after he'd returned to California in '83. They had shared their history in these letters: Wilfred's joy over his adoption, Michael's panic over testing HIV positive, Michael's elation over a new boyfriend named Thack he had met on a tour of Alcatraz. That revelation had stung at first, since Wilfred had nursed a dream that his chaste fortnight adventure with Michael might one day blossom into something bigger. But he got over this puppy love as time wore on. Michael's words on that flimsy blue paper had become something far more substantial than any romance Wilfred had ever known. That's why he kept the letters in an old silver alms box he had found in the Easley chapel. They mattered to him.

He opened the box and removed the most recent letter. Poppy Gallagher had brought it directly from the post office when she dropped off the place cards. She knew these airmails from San Francisco were important to him. He had saved it for now, for bedtime.

He opened it and began to read.

Dear Wilfred,

It's good to know you're reading this, since this has been a shit week for me, and I need to put this into words. My best

*friend Steve just died. He had been living at a Zen hospice in
the Castro where just last week I watched a Bette Midler movie
with him. His room had been cleared out when I arrived there this
morning, since they had to make room for more dying men. He
was the sweetest guy. You might remember that we entered the
Great Tricycle Race together. The folks at the hospice had saved
his beloved Mighty Mouse doll for me, and I burst into tears on
the spot. He was two weeks short of making it to forty.*

*The streets of the Castro seemed full of ghosts today, skeleton
men covered in purple lesions. It was hard not to see them as some
future version of me. I'm still okay, though, despite the fact that
my T cells have gone down like a preacher's daughter. Thack used
to be some comfort to me, but he's strangely distant these days. I
can't tell what's going on with him. Sometimes I think he only
sticks around because of how it would look to others if he left.*

*Let me get to the point: How would you feel about me coming
to visit for a few weeks?*

*I'll write to Mona about this, but I wanted to run it by you
first, since you may be shacked up with that hot vicar's son by
now. I know you're taking in paying guests now, so that may
make for more complications. Just be honest with me. I'd love to
see you both.*

Love,

M<small>ICHAEL</small>

Wilfred's mind was racing when he returned the letter to
the box. He hadn't seen Michael for at least five years, when he
and Thack came through London on a business trip for Thack's
preservation work. They had met at an Indian restaurant in Earl's
Court and had drinks afterward at Harpoon Louie's. They could

have gone to the nearby Coleherne, where Michael and Wilfred had met one rainy spring night five years earlier, but that would have felt awkward—even a little selfish—with Thack along for the ride. The evening was pleasant but curiously formal, and after that Wilfred and Michael had returned to the intimacy of letters.

Now there was this.

Wilfred settled back into the cushions of his sultan's bed and began to map out a plan. Midsummer Day was just around the corner, and that would be a perfect time for Michael to visit. There were bonfires and maypoles in the village, and Mona would "get her pagan on," as she liked to put it. The weather would be fair by then, too. The house would not be dripping.

He fell asleep with the rain lashing against his windows and dreamed of a warm summer day and the well-remembered laughter of an old friend.

4

HER GREEN CONCEALER

Rhonda woke up with a start when Ernie shook her shoulder. He was already dressed in his charcoal suit and standing by the bed.

"Fix yourself up," he said. "Breakfast is in an hour in the great hall. I'm taking my book down to the library."

When she didn't respond, he squeezed her shoulder and spoke more gently. "It's a beautiful day out there, honey. We can take a walk after breakfast."

Honey. She had once loved the sound of that word, and what it meant when he called her that. Now it was nothing more than damage control.

She waited until he had left before going to the vanity to see what he meant by "fix yourself up." The sight of her face shouldn't have startled her, but it did. The flesh of her cheek, which was merely pink and swollen when she took her pill and went to sleep, had settled into an angry red on its way to eggplant. At least he hadn't broken the skin this time.

She reached into her zipper bag and removed her new pot of green concealer, the one she had bought at Harrods when Ernie was shopping for brandy in the Food Hall. She dabbed it on tentatively with a brush, wincing a little as she did so. Green, she knew well, would neutralize the red before she applied her own foundation.

She wondered if Lady Roughton would be at breakfast or whether it was, please Lord, just a self-service buffet. She had considered requesting that breakfast be served in their room, but Ernie had squelched that by leaving without her. She would just have to face the gaze of others on her own again and hope that her concealer would do the trick and the swelling wouldn't show underneath her rearranged hair. She hated the look of revulsion and pity in the faces of her friends when they saw that something was amiss. She wanted to tell them that it wasn't as bad as it looked, that Ernie, Lord love him, just went a little crazy sometimes.

Her heart leapt unexpectedly as she entered the great hall. The golden stained-glass windows were splashing sunshine—real sunshine—all over the room. She knew it was real because the other windows, the clear ones, offered blue sky and green trees, solid proof that a pretty spring day lay just outside. Ernie was already seated at the big table. Wilfred was serving him pancakes from a silver platter.

"There she is," crowed Ernie, looking up. "Come join us, honey, before I eat all of these damn things. This young man makes the best damn pancakes you ever tasted."

She took a seat across from Ernie.

"I can make new ones," Wilfred offered. "It won't take a second."

"No, no," she said. "These are just fine, I'm sure."

"Get you some of this honey," said Ernie, pushing a decanter toward her. "It comes from their own hives out back."

"Don't mind if I do," she said, largely for Wilfred's benefit.

Ernie was always like this for at least a day afterward. She thought of it as the honeymoon period, when he was sweet to her and excessively charming to the rest of the world. He never came close to apologizing, but he had mastered the art of pretending it had never happened. And Rhonda, in turn, had learned to interpret that as sincere remorse. It was really all she had to work with when it came to loving this man.

Lady Roughton burst out of the kitchen with a server of scrambled eggs and sausages. She was dressed in blue jeans and a pink satin cowgirl shirt with pearl snaps. She reminded Rhonda of Joan Crawford in a strange Western she had seen as a girl. *Johnny Something?*

The lady of the manor was in high spirits this morning. "Okay, people, it is one beautiful morning out there, the bird's on the wing and the corn is as high as an elephant's eye." She wrangled a red curl out of her eyes, then glopped eggs onto Ernie's plate.

"You grow corn, too?" Ernie said pleasantly.

"It's a *song*, Ernie." Rhonda wondered if this would sound like backtalk, but it rolled right off him. The honeymoon was definitely on.

"It's just my bad joke," said Lady Roughton, doing her part to smooth things over. Rhonda liked that about this woman. She could be brusque, but she was always kind.

"Tell me this," said Ernie. "What's the prettiest walk around here? I'd like to take my bride on a stroll around the grounds."

She was always his bride after he'd beat her up.

"Well," said Lady Roughton, pulling up a chair across from them. "I'm partial to the folly, but it's a bit of a hike uphill, and it might still be soggy after the storm. There's a lovely bluebell wood just behind the barn, and you could just go with this one."

By "this one" she meant the big yellow dog who had just joined them.

"Nilla!" cried Rhonda, as if seeing an old friend. The dog came around the table to greet her. Her instinct was to reach out to pet her, which was a mistake, since Nilla took that as an invitation to leap on the arm of the chair and drag her huge tongue across Rhonda's face. "Oh, dear," she said, pushing the dog away.

"She's bad about that," said Lady Roughton. "She just decides that somebody needs a kiss and gives it to them."

"She certainly does" was all Rhonda could manage. She tried to sound amused, but she was immediately wondering if that concealer was truly waterproof as advertised, or if her face was now ablaze with her technicolor shame. She studied Lady Roughton's face for an answer, but saw no pity there, no revulsion. She didn't look at Ernie, because he was already roughhousing with Nilla, and he would have pretended not to notice anyway.

It was not until later, when she checked her face in the vanity mirror back in the room, that she wondered if Nilla just liked the taste of makeup. Or she had sensed in some deep-down doggy way that Rhonda had a wound that needed licking? In either case she was relieved to see that her green concealer had stayed put.

She was ready for that walk in the bluebell wood.

5

SHELL-SHOCKED

W ilfred was trimming buds in the greenhouse when Mona finally found him. She was glad the Blaylocks were off in the wood and wouldn't wander in here asking questions. Some of her guests would no doubt be impressed by this sight, but something told her the Blaylocks would not be among them. A lot of local folks knew that Mona grew weed, and really primo weed at that, but she usually kept it on the down low with her guests. It was hard enough to break the news to Mr. Hargis when she made up her mind to do this. He finally acquiesced by appointing himself Greenhouse Guardian, swearing a solemn oath that the Old Gypsy would never come in here.

"There you are," said Mona, as Wilfred looked up from his troweling. "I've been meaning to ask you something."

"Shoot."

"Did you get a letter from Michael?"

Wilfred set down his trowel and put a hand on his hip. "You know I have because your little snuggle bunny delivered it to me."

"Do not call Poppy my little snuggle bunny." She was smiling in spite of herself. Wilfred had a way of cutting to the chase.

"So it's girlfriend now?"

"It's not anything. Poppy is my *calligrapher.*"

Wilfred laughed. "You're gonna hafta start paying her if you want us to believe that."

"You are seriously deluded, my child. And *you* know nothing about love when it comes to women. So what did he say?"

"What did who say?"

"Michael. In his letter."

"Oh . . . he was depressed that his best friend had just died."

Her gut still clenched when she heard things like this. "*Who?*"

"I don't think you'd know him. He's a recent friend. They sang in the Chorus together. Remember that bloke who entered the Tricycle Race with him?"

"Oh yeah." She felt ashamed to be relieved that she hadn't actually known the dead guy. She had remained braced for the worst ever since Michael had tracked her down here to tell her that Jon Fielding had died. That news out of nowhere had totally clobbered her, since she had never even known Jon was sick, but he would be only the first of many friends to die in the pandemic. There are five or six other guys in San Francisco, old disco buds mostly, and her yoga instructor in Seattle, her last city before blowing the American pop stand for England.

And, of course, there was Teddy—Lord Edward Roughton—the man she had married so he could fulfill his dream of being sexually free in San Francisco. The whole thing had been arranged by a British marriage broker in Seattle. She had gladly given Teddy her hand, and the green card that came with it, since she knew how good it felt to be yourself in San Francisco.

Unless, of course. Unless.

Teddy came down with AIDS four years after moving to the city and died a year later. They hadn't corresponded at all, since they hadn't really been friends, but he had sent her a sort of thank-you Polaroid when he was still healthy. He was sitting in a bar, decked out in black leather from head to toe as he toasted her with some preposterous umbrella cocktail. He looked goofy as hell but undeniably happy, and that was good to know, at least. She kept the Polaroid above her desk until it faded to a sickly gray, reminding her too often of how Teddy himself must have gone.

It was agony to keep losing people in absentia, but Easley was home now—her "forever home," to use the term Ollie Bunting had used when offering up his beloved Nilla for adoption. Ollie, a caterer who lived in Bourton-on-the-Water, was the first person with AIDS she knew around here, though there would certainly be more to come. The Cotswolds were just too pretty not to have gay boys tucked into every nook and cranny.

When Ollie secured a place to die at the London Lighthouse, he realized Nilla could not come with him, so Mona had promised a forever home to a dog, something she had never even promised to a human. And one day, on a whim, when Ollie was close to the end at the hospice, she had loaded Miss Vanilla Wafer into the Toyota for the two-hour drive into London. To witness the dog's ecstatic reunion with a blind man covered in lesions was almost too much for her. But you had to have last visits for the sake of the still-living.

Wilfred had noticed the cloud that had come over her face.

"What is it, Mo?"

"Did Michael ask about coming to visit?"

"Yes! He wrote you too then? Super, innit?"

She couldn't celebrate just yet. "He's still okay, isn't he?"

Wilfred shrugged. "Seems to be. Except for some issues with Thack."

That was nothing new. Mona's last phone call with Michael had been about his ever-more-distant boyfriend. "I was just afraid that he was coming . . . you know . . . to say goodbye."

"Oh Mo." He smiled at her wanly and gave her one of her curls a flip. "Mother Worrywart."

"I know," she sighed, since there was no use in denying it.

"He just wants his friends," said Wilfred. "And that's us."

And with that, her early days with Michael rolled through her head like an old newsreel: Michael getting dumped by that Marine recruiter and moving in with her at 28 Barbary Lane. Michael refusing to strip at the nude beach, because he wanted to preserve his tan line for the baths. Michael crying in her arms at the Jockey Shorts dance contest when Jon Fielding walked out of the bar in disgust. Michael when she called him Mouse.

"When shall we invite him?" she asked, her anxiety melting away.

"I was thinking Midsummer Solstice."

"Perfect! The roof won't be leaking."

He laughed. "We do think alike."

"This is just wonderful, Wilfred!"

"Finally the white lady gets it."

"He still looks healthy, doesn't he? Has he sent you any snaps?"

"You are hopeless, Mo."

"I am shell-shocked is what I am. I've got guys dropping all around me. Answer the goddam question, please."

"Yes, I've seen snaps. And yes, I'd still fuck him."

She gave him her best deadeye. "I don't believe that's what I asked."

He plunged her trowel into a pot and gave her a wicked smile. "But isn't it reassurin'?"

6

THE BLUEBELL WOOD

It was good to have Nilla along for their walk. She would run ahead of them through that supernatural carpet of flowers, and Ernie would delight in her every whim.

"Look at her go! She knows what she's doing, that girl! I bet she knows every creature in the woods and where they live. Goddamn, she's amazing. Just look at that."

As usual, Ernie was at his most endearing when talking about a dog, though Rhonda knew that right now he was only doing it to keep from talking to her. "And just look at these bluebells," she said, hoping to divert him. "They aren't really blue at all, are they? They're violet, and they're almost glowing under the trees. They're . . . what's the word? . . . *iridescent*."

"Damn if they aren't," said Ernie, and he stopped to hold her hand for a moment, catching her by surprise. "Doesn't this remind you of going to Orton?"

Orton was a white-columned plantation house in North Carolina that was open to the public. She and Ernie drove down every year to look at the azaleas, which were gorgeous but never the color of bluebells, and never this sweetly scented, of course. Still, Ernie was using flowers as an opener, and that was something. His heart was still there, underneath.

He squeezed her hand. "We've had some sweet memories, haven't we?"

"Yes, we have," she answered quietly.

"And I hope you know how much you mean to me and the kids."

He always brought up the kids during the honeymoon period, though they were grown-ups now and living with their own families in other cities. They were his reinforcements whenever she seemed on the verge of leaving him.

She let go of his hand. "I need you to tell me you're sorry, Ernie. I need you to say it."

"Oh, don't start harping on that again!"

"Then don't ever do it again."

"For Christ's sake, Rhonda. Do you think I *like* doing it? Do you think I like seeing you like this?"

Her hand flew to the side of her face. "It's *showing*, you mean?'

"No. No one can tell. You look fine, honey. You're still my beautiful bride."

They walked together in silence until they came upon a bench and sat down. There were bluebells in every direction.

"You know," said Ernie after a while. "We could avoid this every single time if you just wouldn't push my buttons the way you do. You know how I get. If you hadn't insisted on bringing up Jesse—"

"I was trying to make you feel better, Ernie."

"Well, you didn't, did you?" He was still calm but looking

directly into her eyes. "You deliberately provoked me. You enjoy it."

"Ernie . . . It's my instinct to make things better if I can. I'm your wife. I just wanted to get to the bottom of what's hurting you." She hesitated, then took the plunge. "It's not just about an invitation to the Senate cafeteria, is it?"

"What do you mean?"

"Have you and Jesse . . . broken up?"

"*Broken up?*"

"As friends, I mean. Colleagues, whatever. You were always squabbling on the phone."

He drew himself up, "We did not squabble. We had differences of opinion sometimes. Men do not squabble. This was a goddamn election campaign."

"Okay . . . so when was the last time you spoke to him?"

"How could I possibly know—?"

"He was your friend, Ernie, and now he's not, apparently. When did that happen? How did that happen?"

"How the hell would I know?

She took that in for a moment. "So it was his doing, not yours."

This was more of a statement than a question, and Ernie left it there, unacknowledged.

"I know very little about male friendships," she went on, "but I do know that men can just as easily feel jilted as—"

"*Jilted?* By Jesse? He drew back and laughed. "This is some more of that Oprah shit, isn't it? How long are you going to let that woman fill your head with nonsense?"

They sat there in silence for moment. Then she began again. "My point is . . . I can understand how you must be hurt. You worked so hard for Jesse, so . . . his silence must be baffling to you. I just don't you want you to take it personally."

There was total silence as Ernie gazed at the ground beneath his knees. Finally he said: "Just drop it."

"I just think—"

"Did you hear me, Rhonda?"

She knew this was the end of any further discussion, so she retreated into the safety of flowers. "You know they say these bluebell woods only occur in the most ancient forests. They have an actual ancestry, these flowers."

"Who says that?" He was looking at her now, glowering.

"Well . . . Lady Roughton."

He snorted. "I don't trust a word that wacko says."

"That's not fair, Ernie. She's just a free spirit."

"She called this dog a lesbian." Nilla had returned to solicit a few head rubs from Ernie. "Did you catch that? What was that about?"

"It was just a joke of some sort."

"A pretty damn dicey one, if you ask me. Makes me wonder about her."

"She had a husband, Ernie, and they were very much in love."

She wasn't sure if this was true, but she wanted it to be. She wanted to believe that *someone* could know true love in this fairy-tale landscape. She wondered how it would feel to sit on this bench, afloat in the heady perfume of bluebells, with a man who cared for her deeply. Lady Roughton must have known that feeling, however briefly, once upon a time.

———

They walked back to the manor house in silence, following the same narrow pine-bark path that had brought them there. "Bluebells are delicate creatures," Lady Roughton had explained before this outing. "Once they're trampled, it takes them a long time to recover."

I know about that, thought Rhonda.

As they neared the barn, an old man in a tweed cap stepped out of the shadows to greet them. "Top o' the morning," he said, touching the bill of his cap. "I trust the bluebells met with your approval."

"Oh, yes," said Rhonda. "So lovely."

"Very nice," said Ernie.

The old man took a step closer. He had a lazy eye, Rhonda noticed, and a complexion like corned beef. "Folks always ask what I did to make 'em grow that way, but they're strictly God's doing. They've been growing in these woods for nigh unto four hundred years."

Rhonda shot a look at her husband. *So there.*

"Say," said the old man, "you didn't happen to see an old man up there? About my age with a ring in his ear?"

They both shook their heads.

"A swarthy fellow." He leaned forward and lowered his voice, as if about to convey a secret. "These Gypsies will steal the land from right under you, if you let 'em."

Ernie frowned. "You have Gypsies around here?"

"Not if I see 'em first. A groundskeeper's duty is to defend against foreign invaders."

Ernie chuckled in appreciation. "Good man."

Rhonda asked him how long he'd been the groundskeeper at Easley.

"Oh . . . since Jesus was a baby, some say. Or at least since Lord Teddy was." He touched his cap again. "Let me know if I can be of any assistance. I'm in charge of the outdoors around here."

They thanked him and continued on their way.

"He's a sweet old thing," said Rhonda.

Ernie nodded in agreement. "First sane person we've met since we got here. A real salt-of-the-earth fellow."

Rhonda figured that remark about foreign invaders must've won Ernie's heart.

B ack at the house Ernie retired to the library with his Tom Clancy book, so Rhonda decided to run another tub. She took care not to get her head wet, though, since she didn't want to have to do repairs to her green undercoat. As she lay there inhaling the elixir of the lavender bath salts, she realized that the bruise was actually throbbing.

She could feel her heart beating in her face.

This was worse than the last time, she realized, almost as bad as last Christmas. There was just no thinking about it anymore, no easy rationales. Some dam inside her had finally burst and swept her onto the shores of what had to be done. It was almost a relief.

She rose from the tub and dried off with one of Lady Mo's enormous bath towels. Then, very gingerly, she applied cold cream to her face and removed both layers of makeup. There were livid new colors raging beneath the green camouflage.

She dressed in slacks and a blouse and went to the bedside phone, dialing zero for the house. It rang eight or ten times before someone picked it up.

"Easley House."

"Wilfred?"

"Yes, Mrs. Blaylock."

"Is your mother around?"

"Sure. She's here setting up for dinner."

"Could you please ask her to come to my room right away."

"Certainly."

"And make sure that my husband doesn't see her."

"Okaay."

That sounded tentative, so she added: "That part's very important, Wilfred."

"I understand, Mrs. Blaylock."

She hung up the phone and began throwing clothes into her suitcase.

7

WE GIRLS

It was well past teatime when Ernie Blaylock emerged from the library and headed upstairs to the bedroom. Mona heard his leaden footsteps on the stairs and wondered how long it would take him to return. Less than two minutes later he had tracked Mona down in the kitchen, where she was presiding with casual aplomb over a pot of chicken soup.

"Have you seen my wife, Lady Roughton?"

"No," she replied calmly, without looking up. "Not since you left for the bluebell wood."

"She's not in our room. I don't where else to look."

"Well . . . she said something about wanting to visit the folly. You know what . . . I'll bet Wilfred has seen her in his travels." She went to the swinging door and bellowed Wilfred's name into the great hall, where her son was already waiting with bated breath.

"Yes, Mo?"

"Will you come in here, please?"

Wilfred came bounding through the door.

"Mr. Blaylock here seems to have mislaid his lovely wife. I told him you were bound to know where she was."

"Oh, well . . . sure. She went into the village."

Mona threw up her hands as if to say "problem solved."

Ernie Blaylock looked satisfyingly thrown.

"She said you'd be joining her later in the tearoom," Wilfred added. "She wanted to do some shopping on her own first."

Mona widened her eyes playfully. "We girls know how *that* is."

"How far is the village?" asked Blaylock.

"Not far. Barely half a mile," replied Wilfred.

"It's walkable," Mona said.

Blaylock's brow furrowed. He rushed out of the kitchen and clomped up the stairs.

Wilfred glanced guiltily at Mona. "Did I fuck up?"

"No, lamb. You're doing fine."

Blaylock was beet red when he returned moments later. "I checked! Her luggage is gone!" He turned to Wilfred with a scary ferocity. "Did she have it with her when she left?"

"I . . . I don't really remember, actually."

"Why would she take her luggage with her if she was just going into the village?"

"Well," Mona offered, "some ladies like to keep their personal things nearby, especially if they're on the road and—"

"She might have caught a cab, come to think it. I told her about the souvenir shop in Moreton-in-Marsh." Wilfred was trying, unsuccessfully, to bail her out.

"And why would she need her luggage in . . . Moreton Whatever?"

"For the souvenirs?" suggested Wilfred.

"Or the train," said Blaylock ominously.

Mona and Wilfred swapped a quick glance. Then Mona checked her watch.

"Why did you do that?" asked Blaylock.

"Do what?"

"Look at the time."

"Oh . . . force of habit, really. Guests heading back to London usually try to catch the three o'clock train. Which is not to say that *she* did that, but—"

"What time is it now?"

"Uh . . . a little after three."

"She's on that train, isn't she?" There was an accusatory tone in his voice.

"I know nothing of the kind. I'm just speculating. Do you know why she might have *wanted* to get on that train?"

Blaylock just glowered at her.

"If you two had a lovers' spat, chances are she's off pouting somewhere. We girls can do that sometimes, you know." She was pushing it here, she realized, but she was also rather enjoying herself. She had this asshole twisting in the wind.

"You're not taking me seriously," he said, "and frankly I resent the hell out it. I'm deeply concerned about the safety of my wife."

"Of course you are," said Mona with a poker face.

Wilfred was already suppressing a giggle.

"And if you're really that worried we can call an excellent constable who lives just down the road. She snapped her fingers at her son. "You know . . . what's his name, Wilfred?"

"Uh . . . Inspector Dalgleish?"

"That's the one!" As usual, Wilfred was a lousy fabulist, but she was fairly sure that this asshole wasn't familiar with the novels of P. D. James. "Dalgliesh is the best in the county, she added. "I'm sure he'd be happy to file a missing person report."

"That's not necessary," muttered Blaylock, looking decidedly uncomfortable.

"Then why don't you let us set up a lovely tea in the library. You can relax with your Tom Clancy until Rhonda returns with her suitcase full of Cotswold souvenirs. There's no point in stressing about this, Mr. Blaylock. I'm sure she'll be back."

"Not if she's on that train."

"Well, if that's the case, there's another train to London at six, and we can drive you to the station ourselves. You've paid for two more nights here, but . . . I'm afraid we can't offer you a refund. I'm sure you understand."

So they left Blaylock in the library with a bottle of brandy and a mountain of finger sandwiches and waited for the afternoon to wear on. When Rhonda didn't appear after two hours, Wilfred went into the room to inform the now slurry-drunk Blaylock that his wife had phoned from London. Mona had just taken the call upstairs.

"London," repeated Blaylock.

"Yes sir. Victoria Station. She called as soon as she got in."

"That's thoughtful of her. Did she shay why she had gotten on the goddamn train in the firsh place?"

"No, but . . . she said you would know."

That shut him up, briefly.

"Oh, and she said that if you want to know her plans from now on out you should check in with her sister Cindy in . . . Tarboro, was it? Is that a place?"

"That's where we live!" barked Blaylock.

"Oh . . . sorry. Sounds lovely, though."

The drunken guest reared back like an adder about to strike. "Donshoo sass me, you stuck-up British pickaninny!"

Wilfred gave him a curdled smile. That was certainly a new one.

"Well . . . righty ho, then. I'll have a cab for you straight away, Mr. Blaylock. We don't want you missing that six o'clock train, do we?"

The driver who took him to the station was Colin, the same driver who had brought the Blaylocks to Easley twenty-four hours earlier. As the car pulled out of the driveway, Wilfred and Mona stood by the side entrance and waved goodbye, smiling broadly as they murmured under their breath.

"So long, asshole."

"Adiós, motherfucker."

They looked at each other and laughed.

"I'm so proud of us," said Mona.

"Yeah?"

"We're a goddamn *team*!"

"Plus we just made a thousand bleedin' quid in one day."

"Well, true enough, but—"

"That's doin' it the hard way, I know."

Mona put her hand across her son's shoulder. "Why don't we celebrate tonight? Take a picnic up to the folly, smoke a little weed . . ."

"You're a mother after me own heart."

"I'm an impossible bitch, is what I am, Wilfred. I'm sorry I gave you shit about the minstrels' gallery. If you hadn't done that, we would never have—"

"Oh shit," said Wilfred, suddenly remembering what she was remembering. "I'll go tell her the coast is clear."

So he hurried into the house and up the staircase and through the little door leading to the minstrels' gallery, where he found Rhonda reclining on the cot he'd installed that afternoon. She sat up when she heard him come in. "He's gone?" she asked.

Wilfred nodded. "He's gone."

"You know," she said. "It's really very comfy up here. I've been snug as a bug in a rug all afternoon. It's the perfect hideout."

"It's me fav," said Wilfred.

8

SCRUMPY DOES THE TRICK

Mona's awful father had become a wonderful mother. That was her usual way of explaining how the man who had left when she was a child in Minneapolis had miraculously reincarnated as her landlady in San Francisco. People seemed to understand it that way, even those who were still uncomfortable with the idea of a sex change. Andy Ramsey had become big-hearted Anna Madrigal, the perfect mother to so many people who passed through her old house on Russian Hill. And Mona, of course, could claim biological kinship.

Anna was seventy-three now. Recent photos revealed that she had stopped dyeing her hair and let it gleam like fine silver, though her lipstick was still red enough to stop traffic and she had shown no signs of ever abandoning her caftans. Mona had not seen her for years, but they sometimes splurged on phone calls when the time was right. That usually meant late afternoon at Easley, when it was morning in San Francisco and Anna was making coffee at Barbary Lane.

"Good morning, old lady!"

"Mona! How's things at the castle?"

"It's not a castle. I've told you that a thousand times."

"And I've seen pictures, dear. Don't lie to me."

Mona chuckled. "How's life at *your* castle?"

"Well . . . very much the same but different. Jorge, poor child, has written a letter to Clinton asking that he not be deported. Billy got a job clerking at City Lights. Margo and Justine have brought in a feral collie to save their marriage."

"A feral collie?"

"He's pooping in the corner where I grow my sinsemilla. That's feral in my book. Oh . . . and Tabatha has glued several hundred tampons to the wall of your old apartment."

Mona laughed. "She's the artist, right?"

"That remains to be seen. She's painting them rainbow colors."

Mona laughed. She loved getting these updates, because they meant that Anna was finding fulfillment with her latest logical family. Mona barely kept up with the names, though, since she was never likely to meet these people, and she couldn't help but be a little jealous of the diurnal connection they had to Anna. The original logicals were scattered to the four winds: Mary Ann in Connecticut with a dull Republican husband, Michael across town with an increasingly quarrelsome boyfriend. Only Brian and his ten-year-old, Shawna, remained at 28 Barbary Lane. Mona, of course, was the furtherest away, but she had never felt guilty about that, just a little sadness sometimes that she couldn't pop downstairs whenever she wanted for a glass of sherry in Anna's parlor.

"So Michael's coming to visit," said Anna.

"Yes! I'm so stoked! It's been years. You could come with him, you know."

"I know that, dear. And I will someday."

No you won't, thought Mona. *You've got your comfy old house and your adoring new brood and you aren't about to upset that applecart.*

"You're gonna miss a kick-ass pagan ritual," she added.

"I have no doubt," said Anna. "Do take lots of pictures."

"And I want you to meet my son."

"Well, I want that, too, very soon. He's become quite a strapping young man, hasn't he?"

Mona realized her pitch had begun to sound pathetic, so she abandoned it altogether. "I'm sorry to ask this, Anna, but am I the only one here who wonders if each phone call . . . you know, could be our last?"

"Because I'm old, you mean."

"No! You're immortal! I could easily go before you do. I probably will, in fact. It's just that we're on different sides of the world, and random shit happens all the time . . ."

"Well, that's true no matter where we are."

There was no way she could argue with that.

"You're a worrywart, Mona. Always have been."

Mona smiled. "My son used that word on me yesterday."

"Well, tell him his grandmother thinks he's a very wise young man. What's he up to these days?'

"Oh, still helping me run the house. Still looking for love in all the wrong places."

Anna chuckled.

"And right now he's helping me with a wounded creature we've brought in."

"What sort of creature?'

"An American tourist whose husband just beat the shit out of her. Right here in the house. We're giving her shelter for a while."

"How awful! He's not still there, is he? The husband?"

"No. Wilfred and I faked him out. He's back in London. He doesn't even know she's still here. You would have been proud of us, Anna."

"I'm always proud of you, dear."

"I know that. I do."

There was a long silence. Mona felt on the verge of tears.

"Listen," she said finally. "Don't give Michael any joints for the road. It's risky these days. And I've got plenty of good stuff here."

"As good as mine?"

"Almost. But I'm working on it."

Anna laughed. "Talk to you soon, dear heart."

"Yes. We will. I love you."

When Mona hung up, Cole Porter provided his usual commentary for the moment:

How strange the change from major to minor, ev'ry time we say goodbye.

They had given Rhonda a new room, a smaller one down the hall that wouldn't remind her of that terrible last night with her husband. This room looked out on the Easley chapel and the green fields beyond, so Rhonda had pulled up an armchair next to the window.

"Knock knock," said Mona from the door.

Rhonda jerked her head around like a startled rabbit. "Oh . . . come in, Lady Roughton."

"Sorry to startle you."

"No, no. Not at all. I was just lost in this beauty, drinkin' it in."

It was charming how she sometimes dropped her *g*'s, Mona thought.

"How's that noggin doing?" she asked.

Rhonda turned her damaged side toward Mona. "Still 'Phantom of the Opera,' she said. "I should put my concealer back on."

"Nope. Don't you dare. Your face needs to heal in the open air. Besides, it's just family here. There are no fancy dress balls coming up."

"But shouldn't I just—?"

"Glop on some more of that green shit? No way. My friend, who's a doctor, says that aloe vera is the only way to go. It's nature's perfect healer." (Doctor was stretching it, of course, but it sounded better than "my friend who's a postmistress/calligrapher.")

"Can I buy that in the village?"

"You don't have to. We grow our own right here. Just lie down." She patted the bed.

"I'll be right back."

She dashed out the room and down to the greenhouse, where she snapped off one of the spiny stalks of her gnarly old aloe vera. When she returned, Rhonda was stretched out on the bed, gazing at Mona warily, as she approached with the stalk.

"Rhonda, meet Vera. I know she looks a tad reptilian, but she's very cool and soothing." Mona pulled a vanity stool next to the bed and sat down with the stalk, which was already oozing its magical goo. She dabbed some on the tip of her forefinger. "Now, I'm just going to touch your face very gently, Rhonda. Let me know if it hurts and I'll stop."

Rhonda murmured her consent.

The bruise was a hideous yellow and purple smear. "You have such lovely cheekbones," said Mona, as she smoothed on the balm.

"My great-grandmother was Cherokee," said Rhonda.

"Oh, well, there you go."

"Ernie doesn't like me to talk about that."

Mona stop dabbing for moment. "Well, we don't like to talk about Ernie, do we? Not in this house. This is an Ernie-free zone."

"I'm sorry," said Rhonda.

"And stop with the sorries. What did I tell you about that?" Mona resumed her dabbing. "Anyway, that explains the beautiful brown eyes. Cherokee blood. Lucky you."

Rhonda grimaced. Mona thought she'd hurt her until she realized it was a prelude to silent tears.

"Oh, now. Don't do that. You'll wash away Miss Vera." She snatched a tissue off the dresser and blotted Rhonda's eyes.

"You're just so nice to me, "said Rhonda, blubbering away.

"This isn't nice, this is normal. You're just not used to it."

She broke off another piece of stalk and gently reapplied the salve to Rhonda's face. "So here's the deal: Wilfred and I are having a little picnic up at the folly this evening, and we wondered if you'd like to join us. We can fix you something in your room, but we thought—"

"I'd love to," said Rhonda.

"Great. So lie still and let Miss Vera love your face for a while."

Rhonda did just that, then remembered she'd forgotten to call her sister in Tarboro. She rose from bed and went to the phone on the dresser, where a little card with fancy lettering explained how to make international calls. Cindy answered after three rings."

"Hey, baby sister."

"Rhonda! Are you back?"

"No ma'am. Still in England."

"But I thought you were—"

"I've left him, Cindy."

"Wait . . . what? How is that possible?"

"How is what possible?"

"To leave somebody on vacation."

Rhonda thought it best to stay vague about this. "I had help," she said.

"You must've. Gosh, I can't imagine—"

"Cindy, I need you to tell me you're glad this has happened!"

"Well, of course, I'm glad! I would've been glad five years ago!"

"Really?"

"Yes, really. You know that, sis. I was worried sick you'd end up dead."

"Then I need you to tell him something if he calls you."

A long pause, then a tentative "Okay."

"Tell him I'm back in Tarboro and staying with a friend. And refuse to give him the name of that friend. I don't want him to know I'm still in England."

"Did he slug you, Rhonda?"

"Oh, yeah. But for the last time. And you can tell him you know all about it if he gives you any guff. He won't want a fuss raised."

Rhonda napped soundly after her call to Cindy. She felt something like safety for the first time all day. Ernie had been put off the scent—to use one of his favorite hunting terms—and he surely wouldn't suspect that she had found shelter at Easley House. If he wasn't flying back to Charlotte already, it would be only a matter of hours before he did.

Her afternoon dreams were full of bluebells and birdsong but, mercifully, no Ernie.

She was awakened by a tentative rap on the door.

"Come in."

Wilfred eased the door open and poked his head in. "I brought wellies," he said. Mona says it's still muddy out there."

Rhonda wasn't sure what "wellies" were until he produced a pair of large black rubber rain boots. "I'll leave them here," he told her. "Just put them on over your regular shoes. I'll be back to fetch you in fifteen minutes."

She was dressed in slacks and a warm cardigan and wearing the boots when he returned. (She had resisted the urge to cover her bruises with makeup again, since Lady Roughton would disapprove, and, really, there was no one here who hadn't already seen the damage.) Following Wilfred, she clomped inelegantly down the steps to the greener-than-green lawn behind the house. The hillside that led up to the folly was a steep terraced affair with hidden pockets of mud that sucked on her wellies here and there. The folly itself was a pyramidal cone capping a square open-air room built of that golden stone.

She was thoroughly out of breath by the time they reached the top. Lady Roughton was already waiting for them behind a large circular table filled with picnic goodies: deviled eggs and fruit salad and an assortment of cheeses and crusty brown-bread sandwiches.

"My goodness," she exclaimed. "How on earth did you get all that up here?"

Mona cast her eyes toward her son. "How do you think?"

Wilfred smiled and gave a little bow.

"So sit," said Mona. "That climb is a son of a bitch."

Rhonda obeyed and sank into a canvas camp chair with an audible sigh of relief.

"Want some scrumpy?" asked Mona.

"What's that?"

"Just our homegrown cider. Mr. Hargis makes it with our own apples."

"Is it hard, the cider?"

Lady Mona smiled. "All cider is hard over here.

"Then . . . yes. Please."

Smiling, her hostess plunged her hand into an ice chest and produced a frosty golden bottle, popping open a porcelain stopper before handing it to Rhonda.

She took a swig. The tangy sweetness went down cold but bloomed into a soothing warmth that settled in her bones. She took another swig. "This stuff is delicious," she said.

Mona murmured in agreement. "I've always hated the taste of beer, but scrumpy does the trick for me."

Rhonda felt a rush of unexpected sisterhood. It was amazing how much she had in common with Lady Mona. First Rhonda Fleming, now this.

Ernie, of course, had always ridiculed her for not liking beer. It was un-American, he said.

She was not going to think about him. She would think only about these two sweet souls laying out a feast for her as she sipped her bottle of scrumpy. They each had their own kind of beauty, she thought. In the soft English twilight their complexions had the satiny sheen of porcelain figurines, her Lladrós perhaps, set against a backdrop of distant blue hills.

"That's Wales," said Wilfred, who seemed to have read her mind.

"Really? A different country?"

"Mmm. Different language, too."

"Amazing!" She took another swig of the scrumpy. "Just delicious," she said.

"How about some music?" asked Wilfred. He had a small tape player on the table in front of him. "What's your pleasure?"

"Why don't you pick?"

So he played her a song called "Blue Savannah," a bouncy little tune by an English group that repeated the phrase "my home is where the heart is." It seemed just right for the moment. For now at least her home was indeed on this magical hillside with the moon rising in an indigo sky and the windows of that grand old house glowing down below.

———

It didn't take her long to get tipsy. Actually, at some point after her second scrumpy she had passed tipsy without fanfare and moved into a state of blissful inertia. She didn't even try to fight it. She surrendered to the canvas embrace of her lawn chair while Wilfred and Lady Mona plied her with ham-and-cheddar sandwiches and the most delicious little mince pies.

"Do you make these?" she asked.

"Oh hell no," said Lady Mona. "We buy them in the village."

Rhonda giggled as she regarded her hostess with admiration. "You are so . . . refreshing."

"Uh-oh. The scrumpy's talking now."

"No. Seriously. I mean it. You're the most amazing person. You just say what you think, don't you? I would give you a big hug if I could get out of this chair."

All three of them laughed at once. Rhonda had made a joke that landed with everyone, so she was very proud of herself. For a moment, she actually forgot about her hideous bruise.

She gazed at Wilfred. "So Mr. Hargis really makes this stuff."

"He really does." Wilfred widened his eyes. "But he refuses to divulge his recipe. Prolly cuz he uses dead rodents for fermentation."

Rhonda's horror must have shown in her face, because a sly grin from Wilfred eventually showed her he was kidding. "Oh *you*," she said.

"Can I get you another?" asked Lady Mona.

"If I do, I'll never get down from here in one piece."

Lady Mona smiled. "That's why they call it a folly."

"Seriously, my legs might give out.'

"Then I'll throw you over me shoulder," said Wilfred.

Rhonda tittered, and for a moment imagined that operation: being swept off her feet by this young man who smelled faintly of bay rum, the friction of his strong back against her chest as they bounced down the hill. She blushed with embarrassment, and she could actually feel that blush in her bruised cheek. *No more scrumpy for you, Rhonda Blaylock.*

"You're a charmer, aren't you?" she said to Wilfred. "I'm surprised some girl in the village hasn't snapped you up already." It sounded flirtatious, she realized, but that certainly hadn't been her intention. She was just trying to be nice (and to move off the briefly unclean thought of Wilfred absconding with her).

"I'm not the marrying kind," said Wilfred with a mysterious smile. "I'm more of a Mama's boy."

"Oh, now." Rhonda looked up Lady Mona, who had just served her another mince pie. "That's not true, is it?"

"Not a bit," said Lady Mona.

"I'll bet he has to beat them off with a stick."

Lady Mona strangled a laugh for some reason. Wilfred just shrugged and widened his eyes.

Rhonda hesitated, then took the leap. "Do you mind if I ask you something personal?"

"Sure," said Wilfred. "Be me guest."

"Is Lady Mona your . . . natural mother?"

"I dunno. Does she look natural to you?"

Lady Mona rolled her eyes. "Wilfred, don't be a dick." She turned to Rhonda. "I adopted him when he was a teenager. His father died very suddenly in London. He came through here with a friend of mine, and . . . we took a shine to each other."

"I'm native Australian," Wilfred explained. "Me ancestry, that is."

"Ah." She wasn't at all sure what that meant.

"Aborigine," he added. "With some Dutch thrown in."

"Right . . . how fascinating."

She was certainly glad Ernie wasn't here for this discussion.

W hen the picnic was over, Rhonda made it down the hill
without being flung over anyone's shoulder. Wilfred
stayed nearby in case she lost her footing, then returned to the
folly to tidy up. Lady Mona insisted on walking her back to her
room.

"You've been so kind to me," said Rhonda as they passed
through the great hall.

"Nah," said Lady Roughton. "You've been one of our easiest
guests."

"I can't imagine how that could possibly be true."

Lady Mona snorted. "Well, one of the sweetest, anyway." She
stopped and looked Rhonda directly in the eyes. "You know
you're welcome to stay with us as long as you want."

"Oh I couldn't!"

"Why couldn't you? Are you really that eager to get back to
Tarpatch?"

Rhonda smiled feebly. "Tarboro."

"Whatever. We don't have guests for a month or so, and you
need to heal that pretty face of yours, and you can help out
with things. Something tells me you're pretty handy around the
house. And you can't leave until you see spring come for real
around here."

"Lady Mona, I . . ."

"And cut that Lady crap. It's Mona from here on out."

9

THE GINGER THING

Poppy Gallagher's home had once been a mill that created power for a piano factory. Later, its wheel was used for the production of silk ribbons, another anachronism that had vanished by the dawn of the twentieth century. Sadly, the majestic wheel was long gone, but Poppy's mossy stone cottage remained perched on the edge of Blockley Brook, a waterway barely two meters wide but still babbling heroically in the absence of industry. *Does anything but a brook babble?* she wondered, as she crossed the footbridge to her beat-up old Morris Mini. *Do rivers? Do streams? Are only brooks allowed to babble?*

She stopped midbridge and gazed down at the water sluicing through the low grassy banks and overhanging foliage. She did this almost every morning on her way to the post office as a form of meditation, a calming start to her workday as postmistress of Chipping Campden. It was always pleasantly uneventful.

Today, however, there was a face down there.

A face pale as ivory with parted pink lips and haunted eyes

that gazed up from the rippling water. She had seen that face many times before. She had even studied it at uni. It was the face of her beloved Lizzie Siddal in the famous painting by John Everett Millais.

And there she was in the brook! The inspiration she needed for her next photo show!

She thought of nothing else on the bosky three-mile drive into Chipping Campden. There was a dedicated "art nook" at the post office where Poppy sometimes displayed her photographs for the diversion for customers waiting in line to post packages. Up until now, her subjects had come from nature—old trees, flowers, a lovable fox—and her mini gallery had proven a hit with customers (except for one contentious fox-hunting colonel who had berated her for "propagandizing on Her Majesty's property"). But she had never before tackled a human subject for fear of revealing too much about herself. Portraits were far too personal.

But maybe it was time she got over that. Maybe the depth of her feelings for Mona had become so obvious of late that foxes and flowers just wouldn't cut it anymore.

Maybe it was time for her art to get personal.

It was a slow morning at the post office, so Poppy gave Mona a ring at Easley.

"Good morning, petal. Have the Blaylocks left yet?"

"Not exactly," said Mona.

"What do you mean?"

"I'll tell you later."

"Would you like to meet me for lunch at that new tearoom

in the high street? I have something massively exciting I want to share with you."

"Damn. Can't wait."

That sounded sardonic to Poppy, but Mona often sounded sardonic, so it was hard to read her. "Are you taking the piss?" she asked.

"No. I love it when you're massively excited."

"Good. Then how about noon at the Boscobel?"

Half an hour later, Mona arrived at the tearoom in crisp white slacks and a pink blouse that Poppy had never seen before. "You look nice," she said.

Mona shrugged. "It's finally feeling springy around here." She picked up a menu and perused it. "Is the Coronation Chicken sandwich any good?"

"Haven't tried it yet, but everything's tasty here."

"So what's this all about?" asked Mona.

Before she could answer a waitress arrived to take their order. To keep things simple, Poppy ordered a pot of herbal tea and Coronation Chicken sandwiches for them both. When the waitress was gone, she leaned forward in a way that suggested gossip or even conspiracy.

"Have you ever heard of Lizzie Siddal?"

"It rings a bell," said Mona. "Wasn't she that rocker chick who sang with the—?"

Poppy shook her head. "No, no. Wrong century. She was an artist's model in the 1850s, a legendary beauty who posed for several of the Pre-Raphaelite painters. Some call her the world's first supermodel. You might even recognize her from the paintings."

"Don't bank on it, young lady."

Poppy was tempted to show Mona the postcard she'd brought, but decided to wait until she'd fully made her case. "I've been a massive fan of hers ever since I was in middle school. Completely obsessed with her, in fact, though I knew very little about her beyond her depiction in art, mostly romantic medieval scenes with knights and fair ladies and such. Then I learned about her dreadful life. She came from the working class and was often poorly and addicted to laudanum, like so many women back then. She lost a child, too, and suffered terrible depression. She was my age when she died, exactly my age—thirty-two."

"Where the hell are you going with this?"

"Just listen: Lizzie's husband was Dante Gabriel Rossetti, a painter and poet who was so heartbroken when she died that he wrote poems in a journal that he placed in her coffin when she was buried. But then this sleazy London art dealer, looking to make a few quid, convinced Rossetti that those poems about Lizzie should be shared with the world. So seven years after she was buried in Highgate Cemetery, they dug her up—"

"Jesus! *Who* dug her up? Her husband?"

"No . . . he had a friend do it."

"Well . . . that's what friends are for."

"Mona, please be serious."

Mona mimed zipping her lip.

"Anyway, this friend told Rossetti that when they opened the coffin his wife was still as ethereally beautiful as ever."

"After seven years? That's utter bullshit."

"Yes. It was, I'm afraid. He was romanticizing her in death exactly the way she'd been romanticized in life. And Rossetti himself began to see the heinous nature of what he had done by defiling her grave. He was filled with shame. He was never the same again, they say. It's a real feminist fable, Mona." Poppy was hoping that the f-word would help sway Mona.

"That may be," said Mona. "What are you so excited about?"

"I want to honor her by re-creating the image that most of us know her by." Poppy reached into her shoulder bag and produced the postcard. "That's Ophelia, Hamlet's beloved, painted by John Everett Millais in 1851. When Hamlet killed her father, she became a total madwoman. The painting depicts her singing just before she drowns in a river in Denmark."

Mona nodded as she examined the postcard. "You're right. I've seen this."

"Everyone has. It's one of the greatest renderings of nature in the history of art. All those different shades of green in the overhanging branches and those reeds beside her and that delicate bouquet she's clutching in her hand. It looks very much like Blockley Brook—"

"—which flows right by your house."

"Exactly! It's been there all along. In front of my nose every single day. I don't know why I haven't thought of this before."

Mona nodded slowly. "Now all you need is some other redheaded madwoman to lie down in the brook for a photograph."

Poppy was silent, taken aback by how quickly Mona had read her intentions.

"I'm right about that, aren't I?" said Mona. "Her hair looks red to me."

"It is. It was. Famously so."

By now, Poppy could feel herself blushing furiously, so she was relieved when the waitress arrived with their tea and sandwiches. They were both silent for a moment. Then Mona took a sip of her tea and peered impishly over the top of her sandwich at Poppy. "So," she said, "how long have you been queer for gingers?"

"Petal, please don't."

"It's a serious question. Was I your first Lizzie lookalike? Or just one in a long line of fiery redheaded—"

"Forget I even asked."

"It's like *Vertigo*, isn't it? When Jimmy Stewart gets Kim Novak to dress up like a dead woman so he can—"

"Lizzie Siddal is not a dead woman! Well, she *is* but . . . she's a legendary figure in the history of art. This would be an homage, Mona. Frankly, I thought you'd be flattered."

Mona picked up the postcard again. "She's a looker all right."

"She looks like you," said Poppy. "Surely you can see that."

"I can see that she's—what?—twenty years old. I'm forty-eight, dear girl."

"Forty-nine," said Poppy.

"Whatever."

"But that's the point, don't you see? You'd be Lizzie with the wisdom of a mature woman. Lizzie reborn as a world-weary beauty."

"You'll get a lot more than world weary if you dunk me in that icy stream in a prom gown."

"I've thought all that out. We can put you in wetsuit under the gown. I'll have the camera set up beforehand. It won't take long at all. I've got the perfect lens for it. And we don't have to use it at all if you don't like the photo."

"And if we do? What? Hang me in the post office for a month?"

Her brusque tone stung Poppy unexpectedly. "Do you not like my series?"

"No! I love it! I love the flowers and the little foxes. I just don't know about having my own mug shot up there."

"Oh . . . okay then." Poppy wanted to say that she saw this portrait as a collaboration between artist and model that tacitly acknowledged their relationship. It was no secret around here that she and Mona had a thing going, so why not celebrate that in the name of art? But she didn't dare say that for fear of forcing the issue with Mona.

What if their "thing" was no longer going?

And if that was the case, she didn't want to hear it.

"I'm sorry if I rained on your brainstorm," said Mona.

"No, no. Don't worry. I can find another way to do it."

"There's always Mrs. Benton at the Bake Shop."

Mrs. Benton at the Bake Shop, who was at least a decade older than Mona, dyed her straight, stringy hair a grotesque shade of vermilion. Poppy did not find this funny and said so with her stony silence.

"Hell," added Mona, "do it yourself. You're the prettiest girl in Gloucestershire. Get yourself a red wig. Be your own model!"

Now there was a romantic proposition. Be your own model.

Poppy bit into her sandwich to silence her troubling thoughts.

They walked around the village after lunch, stopping at gardens that caught their eye. They both tried to talk about flowers, until Mona jumped in again.

"I'm sorry I was so touchy about the ginger thing. It's just that I once did the same thing myself."

"Did what?"

"Fetishized someone for a physical attribute—"

"*Fetishized?*"

"Okay, glamorized. Romanticized. Whatever Rossetti did to Lizzie. I did it myself when I was your age. Exactly your age, in fact. And Lizzie's age when she died."

"What did you do?"

"I fell in love with a beautiful black fashion model, and I was so in love with the idea of her—of *us*—that I was devastated when I found out she wasn't black."

"*What?*"

"She had been darkening her skin to get work as an ethnic model. This was the seventies, remember, and black models were suddenly in great demand."

"But she was still the same person inside."

"Not to me she wasn't. She had deceived me, after all. And I suppose she could sense that my interest in her had been more political than personal."

"So . . . what? You broke up?"

"Yes. It was friendly but . . . I learned a valuable lesson. If you love someone for their . . . external appearance . . . they can end up not feeling loved at all." She slipped her arm across Poppy's shoulder. "So level with me. How many ginger mamas have you had?"

Poppy turned to her and managed a crooked smile. "Not enough for you to make it a deal-breaker." That's what Mona was going for, she suspected, a palpable reason to dump Poppy and still lay the blame on Poppy. This really wasn't about hair color at all.

Mona walked her back to the post office but didn't go in with her.

"Don't be mad at me," she said at the door.

"I'm not mad at you," Poppy replied evenly. "Let me know when you want more calligraphy." She knew that was a beastly thing to say, since it implied that Mona only needed her for one thing besides the occasional role in the hay.

But, deep down, that's what she was thinking.

And all afternoon she sat with bowed head in her little cage at the post office, hoping that no one would notice her tears.

10

A DEAD GIVEAWAY

Mona knew she had hurt Poppy's feelings and she felt shitty about it for most of the drive back to Easley. But she knew too that if she'd agreed to be Poppy's model and hang there for a month in the post office, floating in Poppy's brook with a goddamn bouquet of posies in her fist, that the village would have plenty to talk about while waiting in line for their stamps. And they would talk about it with Poppy, too, which of course was what Poppy wanted. She wanted to make their relationship official with a photograph.

Mona did not feel official. Not right now. Probably not ever.

Poppy was beautiful, no doubt about that. Her dewy-eyed Debra Winger looks had sent Mona spinning the first time she spotted her at the post office, but she had proven to be too girly and delicate somehow to have staying power with Mona. Sure, Poppy had recently abandoned her Laura Ashley florals for "artistic" Guatemalan peasant garb, but something about her was still eternally Laura Ashley. That was fine for a night of hot Schoolgirl-Meets-the-Governess action, but in the long haul, it would probably be hell over breakfast.

Mona would probably want to kill her.

Easley was aglow in the afternoon sun when she rounded the bend in the old Toyota. The scent off the jasmine blooming on the gatehouse wall crept into the car on a surprisingly warm breeze. There were swallows swooping in the sky and tender green buds sprouting everywhere, and Mr. Hargis, bless him, had stopped to wave at her from the side of the drive.

Goddamn she loved this place.

She found Rhonda curled up on the window seat in the great hall. Nilla was lying at her feet, looking up at her adoringly.

"Somebody's made a new friend."

Rhonda smiled. "She's been licking my bruise."

"She loves a good bruise. She nearly licked my knee off when I banged it on the staircase."

"She's a born nurse," said Rhonda. "She's a good girl. How was your lunch?"

"Good. There's a nice new tearoom in Chipping Campden. What's that you have there?" There was a book in Rhonda's lap no bigger than a pack of playing cards.

"Oh . . . just my daily devotional. Inspirational quotes. One for every day of 1993." Then, sheepishly, she added, "I haven't looked at it since . . . you know."

"I would imagine," said Mona. She sat down next to Rhonda on the window seat. The golden light spilling through the big window ennobled Rhonda's jutting Cherokee cheekbones. The pain Mona saw there was majestic, almost beautiful.

"It helps me to . . . you know, find peace."

Mona nodded. "We all need to stop and get centered sometimes." She patted Rhonda's knee to show her support. "So what sort of quotes?"

"Oh . . . different things. Some from pastors, some from Jesus."

Oh great, thought Mona. *One of those.* "Well . . . Jesus had some very useful things to say."

That was lame, but it seemed to please Rhonda, who smiled and nodded. "Yes, he did, didn't he?"

Mona hoped to hell she wasn't about to be asked to name her favorite Jesus quote, but Rhonda, mercifully, was already tucking her little book away in her sleeve. "I hope you don't mind, but I did a little tidying in the kitchen. You have to let me know if I went too far. Some gals have a system and don't want it messed with so . . ."

Mona snorted. "It must be abundantly clear that I don't have a system in the kitchen or anywhere else in the house. Tidy away, Rhonda. It can only help."

Rhonda smiled and reached down to scratch Nilla's neck. "I wish we had a dog."

"We do. You do. Right there."

Rhonda smiled feebly. "I meant . . . me and Ernie."

Mona hesitated for a moment. She knew it wouldn't do to scold her about dwelling on her husband, since abuse victims, she had heard, tend to take scolding as just more abuse. "Do you really think a dog would have made a difference, Rhonda?"

Rhonda weighed that for a moment. "No," she said, but at least I would have had company when he was off getting drunk at the club."

Mona looked to see if this was intended as a joke and found the tiniest smile flickering at the corner of Rhonda's mouth.

"That's the spirit," said Mona, smiling back.

Rhonda leaned down to scratch Nilla again. "We had a dog when I was little, but Papa wouldn't let him in the house. He was a mangy ol' huntin' dog who stayed chained up in the backyard. You couldn't cuddle with him or let him sleep on the bed."

"That's so wrong," said Mona. "What's the point in having a dog if they can't sleep with you?"

Rhonda's dark eyes glimmered. "Did your dad let you?"

"Let me do what?"

"Have a dog."

Mona's lip curled. "My dad didn't let me have a dad. He left my mom when I was seven."

"How awful."

"It worked out in the end. And later on I kinda saw his point about my mom. We have to make our own families, Rhonda. You should've booted Ernie out of yours a long time ago."

Rhonda looked far away for a moment. "I figure he's home by now, though my sister hasn't heard from him."

"Just get your mind off that."

"I'd like to . . . but I'd also like to have an ocean between us."

Mona could see the worried look on Rhonda's face. "He doesn't like it when I run away."

"*You've done this before?*"

"Just once. When we went to a Baptist retreat in the mountains. He started slapping me around again, so . . . I caught a

Greyhound back to Tarboro and stayed with my sister for three days. It enraged him like I've never seen before. He felt deserted, I guess. I think it somehow, you know . . . threatened his manhood."

Mona snorted. "Manhood? What manhood? He's a sniveling little worm. What was it, by the way, that made him do this?" She indicated Rhonda's battered cheek.

"Oh just a conversation about a friend of his, a politician he had worked hard to reelect who . . . ignored him after the election."

"And what did you do?"

"Nothing. I sympathized with Ernie. I never much cared for the man, and I told him so."

"Who was he?"

"You probably never heard of him if you've lived here for ten years."

"Try me."

"Jesse Helms. Senator Jesse Helms."

Mona felt her mouth go slack. "You're fucking kidding me."

"You know of him then?"

"Know of him? I despise him. And so does . . ." She was about to say "every other gay person I know" but caught herself in time. If Pandora's box was opened right now, it would surely be too much for Rhonda. Instead she said: ". . . every other decent person I know."

Rhonda looked cowed by the ferocity of this outburst. "I'm surprised you've even heard of him over here."

"We do read the papers, Rhonda."

"I know. I didn't mean . . . I just meant . . . you know, Jesse is actually quite beloved in North Carolina."

"Maybe in Tarbilly."

"No. Everywhere." She turned and looked directly at Mona. "I wish you wouldn't do that."

"Do what?"

"Make fun of Tarboro. It's a nice little town, and it's where I was raised, and some people I love are still there . . . and I can't forsake everything . . . just because Ernie and me . . ."

There were tears tumbling down Rhonda's face. Suddenly ashamed of herself, Mona reached out and took her hand. "Don't listen to me, Rhonda. All my friends say I'm a terrible smartass. I tend to bring a cannon to a gunfight."

Rhonda wiped a tear away. "Are we having a gunfight?"

"No, not at all! It wasn't you, Rhonda. It's just that Jesse Helms has said some awful things about people I love."

Rhonda's brow furrowed. "People he knew, you mean?"

"No, hell no, he didn't know them. But that didn't stop him from judging them in the cruelest possible way."

Rhonda nodded slowly, taking that in. Then, quietly, she said: "People with AIDS, you mean."

Mona was thrown. "Uh . . . yes . . . as a matter of fact."

"Well, that's exactly what I said to him . . . that Jesse shouldn't judge folks who can't help themselves, even if their lifestyle is in violation of God's law."

Oh shit, thought Mona. *Here we go. Lifestyle is a dead giveaway.*

"So you think gay people are in violation of God's law?"

"Well, the Bible says that if a man lies with . . ."

"Oh please, Rhonda. The Bible says all sorts of shit. Do you actually know any gay people?"

"Can't say that I do."

"Well, now you do." Mona fanned her hands out around her face as if presenting a refrigerator on a TV game show. "Ta-da!"

Rhonda gaped at her for a moment, slowly taking that in. "But what about . . . the Lord?"

"Excuse me, but I don't give a fuck about your Lord."

Rhonda winced. "I meant your husband."

"Oh, sorry . . . well, yeah . . . he was gay, too, as a matter of fact, and he died of AIDS. And so did the sweet guy who gave me Nilla before he died . . . and half a dozen of my close friends back in the States whose own parents weren't there when they died because they were oh-so-good Christians and didn't approve of their children's lifestyles. They weren't having life-styles, Rhonda, they were having lives when they died, with marriages and families just like yours . . . well not like *yours* maybe, but—"

She cut herself off when she saw Wilfred come sailing out of the kitchen with a tea tray. How long had he been there? Had he heard her outburst?

He set the tray down on the big table and flashed his best smile. "Can I interest you ladies in a cuppa?"

"No, thank you," Mona replied softly.

"I'm fine," murmured Rhonda.

"Well, it's right here, if you change your mind. And some lovely little cheese bickies I found in the kitchen."

Mona frowned. "They're probably prehistoric."

"I made them this morning," Rhonda said.

"Really?"

"I wanted to make bourbon balls and I couldn't find any bourbon."

"Mmm, bourbon balls." Wilfred arched an eyebrow and settled on one hip. "My favorite kind."

And with that he sashayed out. Wilfred seldom made grand entrances, but his grand exits were often very telling. This burst of uncharacteristic campiness must've been his way of saying that Mona should've included him in her roster of Queers-in-the-Family. He had just taken care of that in a big way, though Rhonda, typically, did not seem to have noticed.

"He's such a considerate young man," she said.

"Yes, he is."

Rhonda's brow furrowed. "If you don't mind my asking . . ."

Mona smiled. "Yep. Him too. Especially him."

Rhonda's frown deepened. "We're not going to lose him, are we?"

Rhonda's use of "we" was what got to Mona. Under other circumstances it might have been presumptuous, but in the moment it felt like sisterly solidarity. She could feel tears beginning to burn behind her eyes, so she left the window seat and went to the big table, returning with the plate of Rhonda's cheese bickies.

"You were so nice to make these," she said, holding the plate out.

"Don't mind if I do," said Rhonda, taking one.

Mona set the plate down and joined Rhonda on the window seat again. "Wilfred is okay right now. He tested negative last month.

"Oh, thank the Lord. I don't think I could take it if I heard . . . you know . . ."

"Yes," said Mona.

"Maybe it's not my place to—"

"No, no. That was a nice thing to say."

She turned and gazed out the window to bring an end to this awkwardness. Mr. Hargis was out on the lawn, moving in his usual erratic fashion. He would stop suddenly and turn and cock his head, as if he had just heard something, or remembered something, then plod off in another direction. He had done this for several years now, ever since his beloved wife had died. Elspeth had been something of a bossy-boots, so Mona figured the old man was still taking orders from her. It was just his way of having company in his garden.

11

MAN TO MAN

Lachlan Hargis was sure he'd seen a shadow in the gatehouse. The Old Gypsy would sometimes lurk there to make sure the coast was clear before heading deeper into the estate. You couldn't see him at all from a certain angle, but you could see his shadow moving on the wall. There was someone there, no doubt about it, but it wouldn't do to shout at him. Lachlan had long ago lost the knack for running, so the intruder would be gone before he could confront him. Stealth was needed here. And silence.

He crept across the lawn, hedge shears in hand, until the gatehouse loomed before him. The shadow was still there, moving slightly. Lachlan decided to call out.

"Who goes there?"

The shadow froze.

"I said, who goes there?"

The man who finally stepped forward was not the Old Gypsy, but one of the guests. It was the nice American gentleman who had taken his wife to the bluebell wood.

"Oh, beg pardon," said Lachlan. "I thought you were some-one else."

"No problem," said the man.

"Just having a stroll, are you . . . sir?" He couldn't remember the guest's name.

"Please call me Ernie," said the man.

"Just being respectful. I'm an old-fashioned sort."

"I sensed that about you when we met. I'm that sort of man myself. Too many folks out there who don't follow the old ways."

"Too true, sir. Too true."

"My name's Ernie, by the way. I bet you have a fine first name yourself."

Lachlan couldn't remember the last time anyone had even inquired. "It's Lachlan," he replied.

"Lachlan," repeated Ernie. "A nice solid man's name. A name you can trust."

"I reckon it is. I hope it is."

"Do you have a wife, Lachlan?"

Lachlan shook his head. "Not anymore. She died a few years back."

"What was she like? Was she a strong-willed woman?"

Lachlan nodded slowly. "That's what they said about her in the village." He didn't mean it to be funny, but Ernie chuckled anyway.

"Tough cookies," he said, leaning closer to Lachlan as if to share a confidence. "That's what the ladies are. They pretend to be weak and helpless, but they end up calling the shots, don't they?"

Lachlan smiled. That had certainly been the case with him

and Elspeth. Even after death, she was still giving him precise instructions.

"I need your help with something," Ernie added. "But first I need to tell you something. Man to man."

Lachlan could see the urgency in Ernie's eyes.

"I'll do my best, sir."

12

THE RUB

Another sunny Saturday had rolled around, so Wilfred had taken the train into London. Mona always felt a sort of low-level anxiety whenever this happened, though she knew that was patently ridiculous. Wilfred was a grown man now—twenty-six, for fuck's sake—and didn't need a neurotic mother imagining the worst every time he set foot out of the house.

"Did you worry about your kids when they were already grown-ups?"

She and Rhonda were standing side by side at the kitchen sink as they washed and dried an entire shelf of crockery. Rhonda, in her diligence, had discovered a few mouse turds up there and was hell-bent on cleaning every dish in sight, even the ones that weren't exposed.

"I worry about them now," said Rhonda. "Especially now that . . ." She didn't finish the thought.

"Now that what?"

Rhonda shrugged. "Now that I'm leaving their dad."

"What does that have to do with anything?"

"Well . . . they still love him, I suppose."

"And they won't love you, if you leave him? That's ridiculous. You're not getting cold feet, are you?"

"No, no. I've made up my mind. I called a lawyer yesterday. I do think it's odd that the kids haven't heard from him yet. Neither has my sister. I called the Dorchester, and he's no longer registered there. It's possible, I suppose, that he just kept following our original itinerary. There was a battlefield in France that he was especially determined to visit."

"Boy, he sounds like a barrel of laughs."

Rhonda sighed with exasperation, but it wasn't about Ernie, apparently. She had spotted some more droppings, and was frenetically scrubbing away.

"You know they only come back," said Mona.

"Who?"

"The mice."

"Aren't you worried about being inspected?"

"God no! Who would do that?"

"I dunno. Whoever certifies manor houses?"

"I'm proud to say we've never let Thatcher's government through that door."

Rhonda sighed audibly. Mona stopped scrubbing for a moment and smiled at her sympathetically. "You poor thing. You thought you were getting a Barbara Cartland novel and ended up with a house full of mouse shit and queers."

Rhonda looked down at the plate she was drying. "Please don't put words into my mouth."

"But you're thinking that, right?"

"Actually, I'm thinking how lucky I am to be here. You're a

good person, Mona. You don't want people to know it, but you are. Frankly, I'm a little surprised you don't have someone."

"Someone?"

"You know . . . a traveling companion."

"Well . . . Wilfred and I had a helluva time in Brighton last summer."

"I meant . . . you know . . . a companion in life."

"Oh . . . that. Why do you ask?"

"No reason. I just think . . . everyone should have someone. No matter what."

"Oh really? And how did that work out for you, Miss Thing?"

Rhonda spoke under her breath. "And there's that cannon you warned me about."

"Well . . . sorry, but the point is . . . some of us just aren't cut out for a one-and-only."

"But don't you miss . . . the company?"

"Sure. Sometimes. And when I do I can call a friend for an afternoon roll in the hay. And have a lovely tea afterward, and she'll go back to her mill before dark.

"Her what?"

"She lives in a converted water mill. An artistic type. Or thinks of herself that way, at least. "You've seen some of her calligraphy."

"When?"

"'Easley House Welcomes the Blaylocks?'"

"The place cards! Those were precious!"

"Well, that's it. She's precious. And I'm not. And therein lies the rub."

"Sorry . . . the what?"

"It's from Shakespeare. Or somebody. It means . . . I dunno . . .

the hitch, the complication. I'm just too much for most people to handle and . . . I've learned to live with that.

"I think that's very sad."

"Why?"

"Well . . . what will you do when Wilfred moves away?"

"He's not gonna do that. He's the heir to this pile."

"But if he meets someone . . ."

"Then we'll move him in with us. Wilfred loves Easley as much as I do. We're a family here, Rhonda. We're not biological, we're logical. We make sense because we love one another."

"I can feel that."

"Good. Then feel it some more. We like having you here."

Rhonda turned and gave her a funny little smile. It was a moment that seemed to carry great significance, though Mona, for the life of her, couldn't tell what it was.

When they were finished with the dishes, Rhonda asked if there were other chores that needed doing.

"Nothing needs doing," said Mona. "Let's go soak up some springtime."

So they roused Nilla from her nest in the window seat and headed out into the warm, fragrant day. "You know what I'd like?" said Rhonda.

"What?"

"I'd like to go to the bluebell wood."

"I thought you already did that with . . . what's-his-face."

"Yes. Now I'd like to do it when my heart's not breaking."

So they walked back to the bluebell wood, settling on the

bench that floated like a raft on a violet sea. Rhonda sighed softly as she sat down.

"You know . . . I pictured you and your husband sitting right here."

"Why did you do that?"

"Oh . . . I'm just a romantic, I guess."

Mona hesitated before leaping. "My husband and I had barely a month together at Easley before he left for San Francisco. And that's where he stayed . . . and where he got AIDS. Our marriage was brokered by an agency in Seattle. I was paid five thousand dollars and travel expenses. I didn't love him, but I ended up liking him a great deal, and I'm glad I gave him the chance to chase his dream in San Francisco. He wanted out of this place so badly."

"Goodness," said Rhonda, sounding overwhelmed.

"I know it's a lot to take in, but it's the truth."

"No . . . I meant I can't imagine someone not wanting to be here."

"Well, neither can I," said Mona, "but that's just us." She turned and smiled at Rhonda.

"Would you like to help us plan the Midsummer festivities?"

"I'd love to! Uh . . . what exactly does that entail?"

"Nothing much. We put flowers in our hair and dance around a bonfire and drink a lot of scrumpy. It's an old-timey pagan whoop-de-do."

Rhonda's brow wrinkled. "Remember . . . I'm a Christian."

"Perfect. We'll have someone for the ritual sacrifice."

"What . . . ?"

"Relax. It's not a human that gets sacrificed—it's a goat. And the nudity isn't compulsory, if you don't want to do that bit."

The light dawned on Rhonda's face. "Oh, you!"

"Yes. Oh, me."

"Do you just enjoy tormenting me?"

Yes I do, thought Mona. *I want to punish you for every casual cruelty that your people have ever inflicted on my people in the name of Jesus. I'm sick of that shit, and you're going to pay for it, because I'm Lady Fucking Roughton and I'm running the show around here.*

She said nothing like that, of course. She said: "Do I like really look like the kind of person who would sacrifice a goat?"

"No," said Rhonda with surprising tenderness. "You look very kindhearted . . . and very beautiful."

"Well, I wouldn't go *that* far."

"I would."

Rhonda was sliding closer to her on the bench with a purposeful gleam in her eye.

What the hell is going on? thought Mona.

13

THE FUCK TREE

London's queer nightlife had shimmied east since Wilfred lived with his drunken dad in their squat in Notting Hill. In those days he would head down to Earl's Court to meet men at Harpoon Louie's or the Coleherne. But now, a decade later, most of the action had moved to Soho, where his favorite haunts were Comptons and the Kings Arms and, sometimes, the Admiral Duncan. They were all within walking distance of each other, and Wilfred loved the way the maze of narrow streets became almost pedestrianized when their crowds overflowed.

As usual, he took the tube into Leicester Square so he could stroll to Soho through Chinatown. He loved the yeasty aroma of custard buns at the Chinese bakery in Newport Place. Sometimes the smell alone was enough to satisfy him, but tonight he craved the sweet, creamy taste on his tongue. He bought a bun at the counter and attacked it in the street, where a tide of manly denim was already surging into Soho on this balmy Saturday night. The air seemed ripe with the promise of unspilled seed.

He decided to go into Comptons first. The rectangular bar arranged the customers like a buffet, so if you ordered your pint down at one end you could see everyone and everyone could see you. That could have disadvantages, of course, depending on the players. Sometimes he got cornered by a bloke he had repelled on a previous visit; sometimes the hope of a frisky evening was dashed by an overeager bearer of bad news: *Did you hear that poor Reggie has gone blind? That Tom Butterfield died last week?* If you didn't want to wreck your fun before it started, strangers were preferable to friends.

There was an especially tasty stranger on the far side of the bar. Except that he wasn't a stranger exactly. His dark hair and luminescent blue eyes were distinctly familiar, though Wilfred, for the life of him, couldn't place him in his pantheon of playmates, real or imagined. He was nursing his beer and pretending not to stare, when it finally came to him. He had seen this man naked and taking a shower, had actually seen water sluicing off his dolphin-smooth chest.

He left his stool and headed over to the object of desire.

"Hey," he called, raising his thumb to show his approval. "Rubber up or leave it out."

The man just blinked at him in confusion.

"Isn't that you in that advert on the telly?"

"Oh . . . yeah . . . that's me. I'd forgotten about that slogan." He was smiling now, at least. He had an American accent, Wilfred noticed.

"That was a very cool thing to do. We need to get out the word about safe sex." Wilfred squeezed past several people and extended his hand. "I'm Wilfred," he said.

"I'm Scott," said the man, shaking his hand.

"You looked good in that advert, too."

"Thanks."

"Never seen an advert with a bloke kissing another bloke."

"Well . . . that may have been the first. That's what I've heard, anyway. Who knows?"

"Was that your lover?" Wilfred tried to sound casual about this, since it was a loaded question. The man Scott was kissing had been every bit as brown-skinned as Wilfred. He couldn't help wondering if Scott might have a type.

But Scott shook his head. "He was just a guy that the modeling agency sent over. We didn't know each other."

"So you're a model, too?"

"Yep."

"Wow." *Good, Wilfred, way to sound like a total plonker.*

Scott ducked his head, looking embarrassed. "It's not that big a deal."

"Must be a great way to meet guys, though."

"Actually, in my experience, most models are straight."

"Really? Well, that sucks. But at least you can come here."

"Yeah. I like this place a lot."

"See anything that strikes your fancy?" Wilfred waggled his eyebrows suggestively. "I mean . . . like . . . in the immediate vicinity?"

Scott chuckled but declined the implied invitation. "Actually, I'm just waiting for my lover right now."

"Course you are," said Wilfred, with only a hint of rue. The good ones might always be taken, but they should at least have the decency not to sit alone at a bar.

"We're having dinner at Balans momentarily."

Balans was the restaurant across the street. Good excuse, thought Wilfred, if it's the truth.

A long, excruciating silence followed. Wilfred noticed that several of the patrons around the horseshoe had been quietly observing this exchange. One of them was smirking. Was that because everyone wanted Scott and nobody got him? Had they enjoyed Wilfred's humiliation?

"Well," said Wilfred, backing away. "Me mate's waiting for me at the Lord Nelson."

There was no one waiting for him at the Lord Nelson, but this seemed like the only graceful way out.

"Thank you for the compliment," said Scott. "About the advert, I mean."

Wilfred nodded and made a beeline for the door.

He walked aimlessly for a while until he spotted a phone box and made a decision on the spot. He pulled a cocktail napkin from his wallet and dialed the number on it.

A familiar voice said, "Hello."

"Rodrigo?"

"Yes?"

"This is Wilfred Porter."

No response.

"We met at the Fridge a few weeks ago."

"Sorry, man. I need a little more."

"I live in Gloucestershire. You drove me to the train in the morning."

"Ah, of course. How you doin'?"

"Good, good."

"We had quite a night." Rodrigo chuckled. "Unless that was the Dennis the Menace."

Dennis the Menace was the name of the E they had bought—
and shared—at the Fridge.

"I kinda thought it was more than that." *Hey, Wilfred. Stop
sounding so wounded. Men don't like that.*

"Are you in Gloucestershire?"

"Actually, I'm in Soho . . . not far from you."

"Damn."

"Try not to sound so thrilled."

Rodrigo laughed. "No . . . I mean . . . I wish you'd given me
some warning. I've got plans tonight."

"Right. Of course. I should've called earlier."

Out on the street again Wilfred considered a drink at the Lord
Nelson and then rejected the idea, since the prospect of chatting
up another stranger in vain was more than he could face. He
wanted instant gratification on this unusually sultry spring evening. He wanted to get his rocks off and get home without any
fuss and bother, and that meant only one thing:

The Fuck Tree.

I t was still light out when Wilfred emerged from the lift at the
Hampstead tube station. It was too early to head for the Heath,
so he crossed the street to the William IV pub—the Willie, as
it was known to its habitués. He ordered a pint at the bar, then
took it outside to the crepe wagon, where he ordered one with
Nutella. The Willie was a shadow of its former gay self—too
many Hooray Henrys these days—but that crepe wagon always
brought Wilfred back for another visit.

He nursed his pint until a silky twilight settled over the village, then headed up Heath Street until the houses gave way to

the heath. The glimmering pewter triangle of Whitestone Pond, London's highest point, lay ahead of him, making his heart race a bit, since it meant that the Fuck Tree was only minutes away, just behind the car park at Jack Straw's Castle.

The pub was a three-story yellow frame building with crenellations along the top meant to suggest the battlements of a castle. Wilfred had never been inside. This evening, as always, he headed into the car park and onto the well-worn path descending onto the heath.

Down here, amid a labyrinth of trees and dense foliage, night had already fallen. He counted several other men presumably bound for the same place. There was really no other reason for them to be here. These woods were already a brotherhood of hungry, unsmiling strangers.

The Fuck Tree stood in a clearing bordered by dark thickets on all sides. The trunk of the tree swooped so low to the ground that it became a sort of chaise against which you could lean for wanking or bend over to be fucked. At the moment neither of those functions was in play, perhaps because, not that far away, a stocky ginger in green gym shorts and a white singlet was setting up a folding table with the brisk efficiency of someone about to sell shortbread at a church fete. He was arranging packets of condoms and lube on the table.

"Help yourself, love," he said, seeing Wilfred approach.

Wilfred took one of each, just to be polite.

"C'mon, you know you need more. I've plenty."

Wilfred smiled. "Thanks. I'm good." He hesitated, then asked: "Are you here in some official capacity?"

The man wiggled a button on his singlet. GMFA: Gay Men Fighting AIDS. "We figured we'd best go to where the action is."

"Ah. Good for you."

"We need a little ambience, though." He reached under the table and produced a large silver candelabra, affixed with six candles, which he proceeded to light with a plastic cigarette lighter. "Wa-la!"

Wilfred was dumbfounded. "Are you serious?"

"Who needs serious? That's what's wrong with some of these blokes. They've got no joy. If you're gonna worship cock in the woods you should be festive about it!"

Wilfred chuckled. "I suppose."

The man lit the last candle and glanced over at the Fuck Tree, where, a trouserless supplicant was already proffering a plump bottom as pale as the moon. Nearby three or four guys stood in a huddle, checking out one another's tackle. "Looks like the party's picking up," he said, just as one of them fell to his knees, having apparently found what he wanted.

"Well," said Wilfred, "I think I'll roam a bit."

"Do that," said the man. "And if you get lost, just look for the candlelight." He saw himself as a sort of hostess at this bacchanal, Wilfred realized, and it was really rather sweet.

"Thanks for the condom," he told the man, though he knew he wasn't likely to use it. He'd been a versatile bottom in his teens, but the pandemic had turned him oral with a vengeance. The conventional wisdom was that the virus couldn't be transmitted by a blow job, unless you have open sores in your mouth. So he ran his tongue around his mouth one more time for good measure, and set off into the woods in search of adventure.

———

The paths leading down into the heath were a maze of leafy tunnels and cul-de-sacs, some of which were already occupied. The protocol here was tricky. If there were several people in a huddle sometimes you would be welcome, sometimes not. Wilfred generally tried to go for the stand-alone guys, since that sort of rejection was easier to handle. If they turned you away, you could bow out respectfully without feeling you had spoiled someone's party.

He had been here only three or four times over the years, but the scene was imprinted on him like a sense memory: the heads bobbing in the shadows, the commingled pungency of poppers and wet leaves, the guttural cheerleading of onlookers when someone was on the verge of coming. It was bacchanalian, sure, but there was a feeling of safety here, too, of brotherhood even, in these deep Shakespearian woods.

He pressed on until he found a nook he could call his own. There he leaned against a tree and got his willy out of his jeans. Several guys approached. One of them dropped to his knees and went down on him, pausing briefly to unscrew a bottle of poppers and take a sniff.

The other one watched, waiting for his turn on Wilfred's willy, which was offered to him in due course by the first man, along with a sniff of his poppers—the etiquette of cock sharing.

The second man wanked himself off with Wilfred's cock still in his mouth. The spunk hit the ground and a corner of Wilfred's jeans. As soon as he stood up the other man moved into place. Wilfred was ready to take a breather, but it seemed impolite not to let him have a go, so he lingered for a moment, making appreciative moans, before buttoning his fly and thanking the man and heading off down the path. He was ready to taste some dick himself.

He found one about twenty feet away: a remarkable thing being brandished by someone in the shadows. Wilfred was so intrigued by its girth and the vein that ran the length of it like a swollen tributary that he didn't look up once to see its owner. He moved toward it and felt its warm heft in his hand. "Nice," he murmured.

"It's yours, mate," came the reply.

It was then that Wilfred finally looked up for a face.

And couldn't find one.

He dropped the cock and fled into the night.

He was out of breath when he finally found his way back to the man with the candelabra. "Are you okay?" asked the man.

"I'm fine," said Wilfred. "Just a little freaked out."

"What is it, love?"

"There's a man down there with his face completely covered."

"How do you mean?"

"You know . . . with a mask."

"Like a Mexican wrestling mask? With holes for the mouth and eyes?

"Yes! It scared the shit out of me!"

The man smiled mysteriously. "I can see how it might. He's a nice chap, though. No danger at all."

"Why does he cover his face then? Is there something wrong with it?"

"In a manner of speaking, yes."

"What do you mean?"

"He just wants to have a bit of fun like everybody else."

"And he wouldn't because . . . ?"

Candelabra Man seemed to hesitate. "Let's just drop it, okay?"

"It's a recognizable face? Is that it?"

"Just drop it, love."

Wilfred smirked. "Is Charles stepping out on Diana?"

The man laughed. "Cheeky."

"Well give me a hint, then."

"I would, but . . . I don't like to engage in careless whispers."

He widened his eyes, underscoring the importance of what he'd just said.

"You're having me on," said Wilfred.

"That's all the hint you're getting."

Wilfred mulled it over for moment. "He does live nearby, doesn't he?"

"Mmm. With a garden that opens onto the Heath."

"Holy shit! I love him!"

The man gave him a sly smile. "I expect you'll be leaving me now."

"I owe you one," said Wilfred as he headed into the woods again.

But this time his masked man was nowhere to be found. Having faced rejection from Wilfred, his playmate of choice, and his greatest fan, this global superstar had apparently continued his quest elsewhere.

It just wasn't fair.

———

He phoned Mona from the train station.

"Where are you?" she asked, with a fretful note in her voice.

"Paddington. I'm boarding in ten minutes."

"Good. I was beginning to worry."

"I knew you would be, so . . ."

"How was your evening?"

"Shitty. One aborted attempt after another. But guess who I almost had sex with."

"Is that the sort of thing a boy asks his mother?"

Wilfred laughed. "It is if I'm the boy and you're the mother."

"And by the way, how do you *almost* have sex with somebody?"

"It's not easy, but I managed."

"You sound disappointed. Are you?"

"Hideously. It was George Michael."

"*George Michael the singer?*"

"None other."

"He was your teenage heartthrob."

"Don't rub it in, Mo."

"Well, it was his loss. You know that, don't you?"

"You're being sweet, but he didn't reject me."

"What do you mean?"

Wilfred sighed. "It's too hard to explain. It's been a weird day."

Mona chuckled. "No weirder than mine, I'll bet."

There was a worrying note in her voice. "Are you all right?" he asked.

"Yeah, it's just that Rhonda's been acting funny."

"Did she try to bring you to Jesus?"

"Worse. She made a move on me."

"What? *She's a Lesbyterian?*"

"We can talk about it later. Shall I pick you up at the station?"

"No. I'll call a cab."

"Okay, then. See you soon, Babycakes."

Babycakes.

The sound of it sang in his head all the way back to Gloucestershire. Wilfred knew that she had called Michael that back in San Francisco. He had actually *heard* her call him that a decade earlier when the two of them invaded Easley unannounced on a tour. He had been a little jealous of it, in fact, the easy intimacy of an endearment that spoke to their long history together. He had wanted that for himself, and now, with very little fanfare, he was finally getting it. He knew it was ridiculous to be thrilled about a pet name. Mona was leaving him a fucking ancestral home. What further proof could he need of a mother's love?

Still, Babycakes meant something important to him, and all the way home in that darkened train car it seemed to keep time with the rhythm of the rails.

Babycakes, Babycakes, Babycakes . . .

14

A MOTHER WORRIES

Mona was in bed when the crunch of gravel in the drive told her that Wilfred's taxi had arrived. She didn't want to appear to be hovering, so after hearing his footsteps on the stairs, she waited a good five minutes before heading down to his room.

"Knock knock," she said outside his room. She always felt a little silly doing this, but you couldn't be too careful. He might have company, after all.

"Come in, your Ladyship."

She found him already in bed—that carpet-draped pasha's tent under the eaves—reading a book by the light of a small, amber-shaded lamp. His head and shoulders had become bronzed in that light. She pulled up a chair to talk to him.

"So where did you meet him? At the Fridge?"

"Who?"

"George Michael."

"Oh . . . no actually . . . I met him on the heath."

"*Hampstead Heath?*"

"That's the one."

"After dark?"

He shrugged a yes.

"Out in the open or in the bushes?"

He smirked. "Do you want me to draw you a map?"

"I want you to tell me you're being safe."

"I promise," he said, raising his hand in a Boy Scout pledge. "I only suck cock."

"That's not what I meant!" He was starting to piss her off. "In case you haven't noticed, Wilfred, it's been open season on gay men ever since the passage of Clause 28. Five years earlier Thatcher's edict against "the promotion of homosexuality" had provoked a rash of fag bashings across the country. "There are other ways to be unsafe, you know. And one of them is wagging weenie in the dark."

"It's not that dangerous. A lot of me mates go there. There's even a safe-sex table with a candelabra."

"Well, that should fend off the fag bashers!" She thought about that for moment. "What the hell is a safe-sex table?"

"You know . . . with literature . . . and a bowl of johnnies, if you wanna fuck."

She rolled her eyes. "And then what? You head off into the woods to wank away?"

Wilfred smirked. "Why are you being such a prig?"

"Because, Wilfred . . . a mother worries." She found herself wincing the moment this came out of her mouth. That was exactly what her own mother used to say when she called from Minneapolis to check up on her prodigal hippie daughter in San Francisco.

Because, Mona, a mother worries!

She was at risk of sounding exactly like that—like good ol' Betty Ramsey, the Republican Realtor from Hell—so she decided to change the subject. "So what did he say?"

"Who?"

She pointed to the poster of George Michael on the wall of Wilfred's tent/bed. "Him."

"Oh." He fidgeted with the edge of the bedspread. "Not much, actually."

"I guess his mouth was full at the time."

He gave her a weary smile. "You're daft."

"Sorry," she said quietly.

"You want details, don't you?"

"A few wouldn't hurt."

"Don't worry. I fled the scene. He spooked me."

"That doesn't sound like you at all."

"He was wearing a scary wrestler's mask."

"What?"

"You know . . . for anonymity."

"Then how the fuck did you know it was him?"

"The bloke with the candelabra told me."

She rolled her eyes at a phrase that sounded straight out of *Alice in Wonderland*.

"You had to be there," said Wilfred.

"*I* don't have to be there. And neither do you, it seems to me."

She waited for a response, but he seemed to be choosing his words. "I just need . . . more men in my life, Mo."

"In large groups? In the woods?"

"Sometimes . . . yeah."

"Not to mention in the middle of an epidemic?"

"Well . . . yeah . . . especially now, when me mates are all dying and the government is hunting us down. I need me fellowship."

She sighed in exasperation. "And I need me son."

He grinned fetchingly. "You have him, Mo."

"Yeah, but I need him alive. Seriously, Wilfred, be careful. You're all I've got."

He took that in for a moment. "It doesn't have to be that way."

"What do you mean?"

"Just that . . . you can let other people into your life besides me. You're so afraid of someone loving you."

She recoiled from this like a slap. "Wow. Where did *that* come from?"

He shrugged. "From your son. Who lives with you and . . . observes things."

"Like what?"

Another shrug. "Like you and Poppy. She asked you to pose for her, and you ran screaming into the night, never to be heard from again."

Again she was thrown. "How could you possibly know that?"

Wilfred hesitated so long that she answered her own question. "You've talked to her."

He nodded. "Just briefly. In the village. She misses you, Mo. She thinks you're done with her."

"She told you this in the post office?"

"No. In the village. At the greengrocer. She looked like she'd been crying."

Mona was cringing. The last thing she needed was an eye-witness to Poppy's distress. She had hoped to make a clean break with the postmistress with a minimum of drama, and now her own son, simply by chance, had made that impossible. "What did you say to her?" she asked.

"Nothing much. I mostly just listened."

"Shit."

There was an awkward silence before Wilfred shook his head and said, "I just don't get it."

"Don't get what?" She was pretty sure she knew what was coming, but she wanted to see how he would lay it out this time.

"She's gorgeous and sweet. You like her. The sex is great . . . from what I can hear from me bedroom. She even has her own cute little millhouse by a brook. What the bloody hell is wrong with her?"

She tried to answer him seriously. "You know . . . I'm not sure exactly . . . maybe it's our age difference. We're just not the same species of dyke. My lesbianism grew out of activism and appetite. Hers seems like something she studied in art school. I think that could be a problem down the line. She's just a little too . . . I dunno . . . prissy at heart."

Wilfred's brow furrowed. "I thought you liked 'em femme."

"I didn't mean that. I just meant . . . uptight."

He smirked. "She doesn't sound that way down the hall."

She glared at him. "Are we gonna hafta move you to another hall?"

"You're bringing her back, then?"

"Bringing her back? I never sent her away!"

"Then call her, and tell her you're not mad at her. She thinks you're done with her, Mo."

Mona studied her son's face for a moment. "What is this, anyway? Why are you so invested in this?"

He smiled sleepily. "I'm invested in you seeming like a good person. Which I know you are."

Mona rose from the chair and wiggled Wilfred's toes beneath the sheet. "Don't be so sure about that."

"I'm sure, believe me." He picked up his book again. "I'm neglecting Stephen King. Why don't you put it before the Jury."

The Jury, as they called them, were a dozen brown long-eared bats that roosted in the rafters at Easley House. Mona sometimes ended her day by telling them good-night, a ritual she kept strictly to herself, since it would creep out most of her guests, including, she felt sure, Rhonda Blaylock. The Jury was her little secret. She drew a curious comfort from them, from the constellation of bright eyes that turned to greet her when she entered the cavernous attic. They weren't afraid of her, and she wasn't afraid of them.

Tonight their upside-down bodies were illuminated by the moon in the window at the far end of the attic. Their huge furry ears, said to be able to hear the movement of a ladybug across a leaf, were folded under their wings. Hearing her approach, the bats made a rustling, clicking noise, but didn't move from their usual positions.

"Don't get up," she said. "It's just me."

There was a little more rustling and clicking, then silence.

"I was just wondering . . . what you think about Poppy."

Total silence.

"Well, you're no help at all," she said.

She walked to the window and looked down at the lawn, where she saw a figure heading into the shadows by the chapel.

It had be Mr. Hargis, but what was he doing up this late?

She waited there a moment longer, then headed down the stairs to bed.

15

NOT A DYKE

It had become customary for Mona and Rhonda to have breakfast together in the kitchen. Rhonda would usually do the
cooking, dishing out stacks of syrupy pancakes with crisp bacon
and scrambled eggs. Sometimes, though not often, Mona would
insist on making her raisin porridge just to give Rhonda a break,
and she was fully prepared to do that today.

But Rhonda wasn't in the kitchen when Mona came through
the swinging door.

Was she still asleep? It was well past nine o'clock, and Rhonda
had always been an early riser.

She headed upstairs to Rhonda's room. The door was open
and the bed was already made. *Had she even slept here last night?*

Returning to the great hall, she crooned Rhonda's name on
the staircase and waited for a response.

Nothing.

Nilla appeared at the bottom of the stairs, cocking her head,
sensing that something was out of the ordinary.

"Rhonda's flown the coop," she explained unhysterically to the dog. "Shall we go find her?" Nilla was always up for a game, if you had the right tone.

They entered the garden on their common mission. Nilla seemed mildly excited but completely clueless.

Mona cupped her hands around her mouth and called out Rhonda's name again. She tried not to make it sound urgent. Just a cheery call to breakfast. She didn't want to convey her growing dread, her sense that something was seriously wrong. And what if something was? Had Rhonda freaked about last night? Had she been pushed over the edge?

She called again, louder this time "RHONDAA!"

Finally, there was a reply. "Up here." It was a child's voice, timid and confessional.

Mona looked up the hill. "At the folly?"

"Yes."

"Stay put. "I'm comin' up."

She bounded up the old stone stairs to find Rhonda slumped in a canvas chair like a despondent rag doll. "What's going on?" she asked.

"I just needed to collect my thoughts."

"About what?"

"What do you think?"

Mona pulled up a chair and sat down next to her.

"It was just a kiss, Rhonda."

"I just don't want you to think I'm . . . like you."

This was a bitch slap from which Mona visibly recoiled. "Oh well, no . . . of course not. Nothing worse than that."

"I didn't mean it like that. I just meant—"

"—that you're not a dyke."

Rhonda flinched. "I would never use that word."

"Why not? It's a perfectly fine word. I use it all the time."

There was leaden silence until Mona added: "So why did you do it, then?"

"Do what?"

"Kiss me, goddamnit!"

"I was just feeling such . . . affection for you. You've done so much for me, Mona. You've been so kind."

"Sorry, but it didn't feel like that kind of a kiss."

"I kiss the ladies in my prayer group all the time."

"And slip them a little tongue?"

"I did *not* do that!"

No she had not. Mona knew she was just joking her way out now, coping with her own embarrassment by vulgarizing what had happened in the bluebell wood. There had, in fact, been something disturbingly tender and soulful about that kiss. She knew very well that Rhonda's intentions had not been prurient.

"I'm sorry," she said. "I know you weren't hitting on me."

"Then why did you flinch . . . and pull away?"

Mona hesitated. "I don't know exactly. You caught me off guard."

"What did you need to be on guard about?"

Good question, thought Mona. The possibility that this hopelessly provincial Christian woman might love her unreservedly? What was she expected to do with that?

"Let's go down to breakfast," she said. "I'll make my porridge."

Rhonda hesitated then said: "I think I should go."

"Go where?"

"Home. To Tarboro."

"Oh, no. Bad idea. That's walking straight into the hornet's nest."

"No . . . my sister is there, and I can stay with her."

"And he'll be there, too, won't he?"

"I don't know that for sure."

"Rhonda!"

"I have to face the music, Mona."

"What music? You've done nothing wrong!"

"I've nowhere else to go."

"You don't have to *go* anywhere. I thought I made that clear."

"But I will, sooner or later. And why stay here? I'm a burden to you, and an embarrassment."

"What in the hell gave you that idea?"

"C'mon, Mona. You think I'm some sort of . . . country bumpkin."

"I do not!"

"Then what are those jokes about Tarboro all about?"

Mona sighed in exasperation. "Rhonda, you are not where you came from!"

Rhonda looked up at her. There were tears streaming down those Cherokee cheekbones. "Then what am I?"

That was the question, wasn't it? This woman had lived with an abusive asshole for thirty years, so there was no one left for her to be.

"Rhonda, you are a good soul, and you deserve a good life." She held this woman's face in her hands.

"But you don't want me here."

Mona gave her head a gentle shake. "Believe me, I tell people when I don't want them around."

"But I've embarrassed you with that kiss, and there's no way we can go back to being—"

"Rhonda, goddammit, this is how much you embarrassed me!" She pulled Rhonda's face into hers and gave her a long, hard kiss on the mouth. Then, standing up, she added: "Now come down to breakfast, you silly woman!"

In the kitchen, they lost themselves in breakfast rituals, with Mona making the porridge and Rhonda chopping peaches for the fruit salad. Neither one of them looked up from the tasks at hand.

"We're almost out of brown sugar," said Rhonda. "I know how much you like it."

"Mmm. I'll have Wilfred pick some up in the village."

"These peaches look yummy."

"Well, it's the right time of year. And the greengrocer likes me."

Rhonda turned and smiled at her. "I imagine everybody likes you."

"Oh, don't be so sure about that. There's a woman two villages away who loathes me with a passion.

Rhonda's brow furrowed. "*Why?*"

Mona shrugged. "She's a toffee-nosed bitch who wants to buy this house and I'm not selling."

"What does that mean?"

"What does what mean?"

"Toffee-nosed."

"Oh." Mona couldn't help but smile. After a decade of living in England, that term had come quite naturally to her. "It means snobby, stuck up. She's an awful racist who won't give Wilfred the time of day. Wait till she finds out I'm leaving the house to him."

Rhonda looked uncomfortable. Maybe, thought Mona, because she's spent thirty years being married to an awful racist. Glancing around the room, Rhonda changed the subject. "Where's Nilla? She's always here for breakfast."

"Good question. She was with me when I went looking for you, but I don't think she made it up to the folly."

"It's not like her to miss breakfast."

"She probably found a rabbit to chase. She gets distracted so easily."

"But doesn't she usually bark when that happens?"

That was true enough. Nilla had a mouth on her, and she used it at every possible opportunity. She had been completely silent all morning.

"She'll be back," said Mona.

16

BEYOND REDEMPTION

Ernie usually woke when the sun hit the stained-glass window and sent shards of colored light into the chapel. The window depicted Jesus, so Ernie felt especially blessed to be woken this way. Never mind that the rest of the chapel suffered from serious neglect, with its stacks of moldy prayer books and garden equipment and God-knows-what-else beneath that mildewed tarp. Such sacrilege was to be expected from the godless woman who presided over this place. According to Lachlan, the last time she used it was when she got married here to Lord Teddy ten years ago. She was truly beyond redemption.

Lachlan seemed a little dim-witted, but he had been very useful. Once Ernie had explained his dilemma—that he loved his wife dearly and was determined to win her back, that he needed a way to stay on the estate until he could make that happen—Lachlan fell completely into line. He believed in love above all else, he said, and helping out his fellow man.

So Ernie was holed up in the chapel, less than fifty yards from the house, behind a dense stand of trees. He could come and go quite easily without being seen, even make forays into the village for food. Lachlan had built him a bed out of two old pews and some bedding from the house. No one ever came to the chapel, so he was safe here.

So far he had seen Rhonda only once. She was heading up the hill to the folly, but even from a distance, he could tell it was undeniably her. And he realized in that very moment how deeply she had betrayed him and how he was going to have to deal with it. He had not loved and supported her all these years to be so readily discarded. She would pay for this. And dearly.

"Ain't that right, missy?

The big yellow dog sleeping next to him stirred and kissed him squarely on the mouth.

"Hey," said Ernie. "You better watch out there. Your missus might be jealous."

He jostled her muzzle. "You like it better here, anyway, doncha?"

The dog rose and stretched.

"You headin' out?" said Ernie, knowing the answer already. "Well be that way, missy. But don't tell her anything."

17

A PERFECT DAY FOR IT

Poppy had spent the morning watching the brook sparkle and dance from her cozy enclosed garden. It was full-on summer now. At least it would be until it decided, on a whim, not to be. That's the way the weather worked in Gloucestershire: its word meant nothing.

So there she was in her garden chaise, soaking up the sunshine while she had it. At the moment she was buried in the latest Maeve Binchy, or rather the latest Maeve Binchy was open across her tummy, while she succumbed to the delicious drowsiness that had come over her like a warm duvet. When the phone rang in the house, she was so jarred that she resolved not to answer it. It was almost certainly someone from the post office with an annoying question, and that would break the spell of her euphoria.

But the phone just kept ringing.

She scrambled out of her chaise and made her way to the phone.

"Yes!"

"Poppy?"

"Yes."

"It's Mona."

"Ah," said Poppy in a lackluster tone. *She wants calligraphy, was her first thought. She has some rich Americans she needs to impress with a menu.*

"Listen," said Mona. "I was a brassbound bitch the last time we talked."

Poppy didn't know what to say about that, so she said nothing.

"I was having a bad day, and I should have recognized what a compliment you we're paying me by even asking me to be Lizzie Siddal . . . and I realized what *fun* we could have with this whole goddamn thing. So why the hell not? What does it matter? All of Gloucestershire talks about me, anyway. Might as well give them their money's worth."

Poppy still wasn't clear. "Does that mean—"

"I'll lie in your fuckin' brook, missy. For as long as it takes to get what you need. I already know you're capable of art, so have at it, Miss Gallagher. I'm yours."

Poppy felt a shiver pass through her that was better than any Maeve Binchy.

"Are you sure?" she asked.

"Didn't that sound sure?"

"Well . . . when?"

"How about today?"

Poppy could hardly believe her ears. This was all happening so fast. "Have you been smoking something, Mona?"

"Do I have to pass a drug test to get this job?"

"Of course not. I just wondered . . ." Poppy cut herself off. She had never expected to hear from Mona again, so why press her luck looking for reasons. Besides, her dream of a lasting artistic tribute to Lizzie Siddal was about to come true.

"Do you need time to assemble things?" asked Mona.

"Things?"

"The dress, the wetsuit, flowers for her bouquet?"

"No, actually . . . I have them all here." It was embarrassing to admit this, since those items had never not been ready. She had bought both the dress and the wetsuit at her favorite charity shop in Stow only days before Mona had flatly turned her down.

"Shall I come over now then?" asked Mona.

"I don't see why not," said Polly, trying to sound casual. "It's a perfect day for it."

M ona showed up in her battered Toyota while Poppy was picking flowers from her garden for the bouquet. When Mona passed through the garden gate, Poppy fell to one knee and exclaimed: "Your posies, fair damsel."

"You shouldn't have," said Mona, in a tone so dry and emotionless that Poppy was pretty sure she meant it.

"Sorry. Bad joke," murmured Poppy. "It's just a prop."

Mona dug into her tote bag. "I brought us sandwiches from the Boscobel."

Poppy was unexpectedly touched. This wasn't the sort of thing Mona usually did. And they were Coronation Chicken sandwiches to boot, like the ones they had in the tearoom before things suddenly went sour between them. Was she trying to say she wanted to start over?

"That's lovely, but . . . shouldn't we wait until after the shoot?"

Mona smirked. "Think I won't fit in my outfit after a sandwich?"

"No! I just—"

"Where is it, anyway?"

Poppy hurried to the sea chest beneath the window and produced the frock she had found at the charity shop, holding it over her arms the way a shop girl would do for a treasured customer. "It's not an exact match, of course, but it's similarly mottled, and diaphanous, and once it hits the water I think the effect will be quite splendid."

"Yes, I think so too."

Poppy gave her a sideways look.

"What?" said Mona.

"Sometimes I can't tell when you're being sincere."

"I know . . . and I'm sorry. I'm working on that. It's no way to be, if we're gonna be . . . closer."

Poppy felt herself blushing furiously. "Well, anyway, here's the wetsuit. Not very glamorous, but of course you won't see it. I just need to keep your torso warm."

"So," said Mona, "this is happening." And with that she stripped out of her jeans and cowgirl shirt. Once freed, her breasts hung low and full against her torso. Poppy enjoyed the sight of them until they were finally hoisted into place by the wetsuit. Then came the frock, which Poppy assisted with, pulling it down over Mona's head and patting it into place.

"This is going to work beautifully," she said, stepping back from her handiwork.

"I wanna see. Where's your mirror?"

"Now now. You said you trusted me."

"Meaning shut up and let the artist do her thing."

Poppy grinned at her. "Roughly, yes."

Mona laughed and let Poppy lead her down to the brook to a spot she had already selected, a tunnel of overarching green that roughly approximated the painting, with spots of blue here and there. Rossetti, of course, had not used a brook at all, since Lizzie had posed in the bathtub in his studio, so Poppy was doing him one better by bringing the scene back to nature. She would be using an old Rolleiflex she had found in an antique shop in Cheltenham. She loved the idea of looking down into an old camera to frame the image; somehow it felt more artistic.

But lowering Mona into the shallow, rapidly moving brook proved to be an inelegant operation. Almost immediately, Mona cried "Fuck."

"What is it?"

"There's a big rock directly beneath my ass."

"Can you move it?"

"The rock or my ass?"

Poppy giggled. "Whatever works. I want you be comfortable. We're going for an ethereal look here."

Mona grunted and removed a rock from beneath her. "Ah . . . better."

"Good. Now I want you to settle back and feel the caress of the water. You're floating down the stream now—"

"I'd better not be!"

"No . . . in the photograph . . . and you're holding this lovely bouquet in your . . . bloody hell!"

"What?"

"It's back at the house."

"What?"

"The bouquet! I'll be right back."

And with that she dashed up to the house, retrieved the bouquet from the table where she'd left it, and dashed back again. She half expected to find Mona out of the brook and mad as a box of frogs, but she was still submerged in the water, gazing heavenward.

"Are you okay?" she asked.

"I'm working on being ethereal," Mona replied.

Poppy leaned down and handed her the bouquet. "Now hold this in your right hand, and with your left hand reach upward. Do you remember the postcard?"

"I think so, yeah."

"Good. That's perfect. You're a natural, petal."

She leaned forward and began arranging Mona's hair in the stream.

"What are you—?"

"Shush," she said, pressing her fingers to Mona's lips.

It was odd to be so in charge like this. She rather liked it.

She fiddled with strands of hair until she achieved exactly the right effect: a great fan of auburn spreading out into the stream. Mona remained passive, immobile. A faint smile bloomed on her face that seemed to be saying something.

"What?" said Poppy.

"Nothing. I'm just feeling . . . happy."

No wonder she hesitated on that word, thought Poppy. She rarely uses it. She had seemed, in fact, dead set against using it. Was this beautiful, passionate, impossible woman finally realizing that love lay as close as another pair of eyes that saw you for who you really were?

"Are you comfy in that wetsuit?"

"Oh yeah," said Mona. "Especially now that I've peed in it."

Poppy laughed and reached for her Rolleiflex.

18

HALF A WORLD AWAY

Anna Madrigal rarely had nightmares, but this one had been a real doozy. When she awoke in her house on Barbary Lane, an image was lingering in her head that lasted all the way through breakfast and beyond. A bout of feverish weeding in the garden did little to relieve it, so she gave up the ghost and phoned Michael Tolliver.

"Now don't think me silly," she began.

"I would never," he said.

"I'm sure it's nothing but . . . I've been fretting about Mona lately."

"Nothing silly about that. Everybody does that."

"I had a dream last night. She was drowning in a stream."

"What?"

"She was flat on her back and the water was rising, and it was all so vivid and real and . . . terrible."

"I'm sure it was, but—"

"I know she wasn't literally drowning. It was just an anxiety dream. But I can't shake the feeling that something has gone wrong over there. That's very real to me.

"Well, you know . . . there's one way to find out."

"We talk on the phone all the time, we have a catch-up just—"

"No, I mean go to visit her. You can come with me when I go next week."

"Oh dear, I'm not much good at travel these days."

"So you're never going to see her again?"

This rattled her. "Well, that's putting it rather bluntly."

"I'm sorry. I just don't understand. I'll make it easy for you, Anna. We'll get one of those geezer buggies at the airport."

"You and Thack don't need that kind of burden."

"Thack's not coming."

"He's not?"

"No."

"Well, that's a shame."

"Is it?"

She didn't answer that. She knew he was fishing.

"You don't like him, do you?"

She hesitated.

"It's all right. I don't like him much either these days. All that anger used to be inspiring. Now it's just . . . exhausting."

She gave a little murmur to show that she knew exactly what he meant.

"So, anyway . . . come with me to visit Mona, the person we love most in the world. And Wilfred, your grandson. You haven't met him, and he's already grown up and gorgeous. And that house is not to be believed until you've seen it. C'mon, lady, don't make me beg."

It occurred to her then that the tables had turned in an interesting way. Ten years earlier it had been Michael who had to be talked into going to England. She had even given him a thousand dollars for mad money, sensing that he desperately needed a new adventure after enduring Jon's illness and death. And if he hadn't gone, he would never have found Mona and the wonderful new life she had built for herself.

"All right," she said, but I don't need a geezer buggy."

Michael laughed. "Who's gonna tell her?"

"Tell her what?"

"That you're coming."

Anna thought for a moment. "Why don't we surprise her?"

"Would she like that?"

"Well," said Anna, "she's always asking me. I don't see why she wouldn't be thrilled if I just turned up on her doorstep."

It was a lovely sunny day in her courtyard, so after breakfast she went outside and sat in her lawn chair. The image that had haunted her dream the night before had already evaporated like a chimera, never to be conjured again. A more concerning issue was why she'd been avoiding her daughter ever since she'd moved to England. It certainly wasn't because she loved her any less now that Mona was half a world away. If anything the love had become more intense when expressed in letters and over the telephone. Had she actually been afraid of seeing Mona on her new turf with new friends and new enemies in orbit around her? What if Mona was different now? Was she simply trying to preserve an outdated memory of her prodigal daughter? And was it actually better not to know if she had changed?

This was ridiculous. How drastically could Mona have changed? She had seen her in the flesh only five years earlier when Mona had rented a villa in Greece on the isle of Lesbos and invited Anna to join her for a month. It was a lovely time of the year, the very tail end of summer, when the rain finally washed away the dust, and the disco down the hill that had once battered them nightly with Madonna had finally been silenced. Mona had met some girls she liked at Sappho's birthplace, and Anna had found unexpected passion with a short, courtly gentleman named Stratos, who might have been a good reason for staying had Anna not had a better one for going home. Back then they all thought Michael was about to die.

But he didn't, and now she was going to England with the still-very-much-living Michael. Death might be final in the end, but it could still be conveniently unpunctual.

Now. What would she need for the manor house? A smart new cloche? A new caftan? It was a pleasing question to consider, since it meant a new adventure, and, as much as she was loath to admit it, she had needed one for a while. Even Barbary Lane could get boring.

19

AN UNFAMILIAR PEACE

Mona and Rhonda spent the morning tidying up the great room. There were new guests coming—a young Mancunian couple on their honeymoon—and the place was looking a little worse for wear. At least according to Rhonda it was.

"I think the mice are back," she said, wielding a broom like a weapon of war.

"I don't think they ever left," said Mona.

"It's so discouraging."

"Isn't it? That's why I gave up years ago."

"You're awful."

Mona grinned at her. "This place has been needing a house-wife."

With that, Wilfred came bounding down the stairs. "Are you putting Rhonda to work?"

"She volunteered. She insisted, in fact."

"That's true," said Rhonda. "I did."

Wilfred looked at his mother. "Is that why you're grinning like an idiot?"

"I am not grinning like an idiot! What do you mean?"

"I don't know. There's just a certain . . . absence of tension in your face. Like life isn't so scary anymore."

"Well, I don't know where you get that. Life still scares the shit out of me. Now make yourself useful and go make up the guest room for our honeymooners."

Wilfred saluted her. "The usual rose petals, milady?

"Whatever you think best."

She hated that he had clocked her so easily, that something in her face had betrayed the glowing contentment that she was starting to feel inside. She had felt it ever since that day she was dunked in Poppy's creek. A sort of unfamiliar peace with the world. It had been easy enough to consign Poppy to the role of occasional sexual playmate—a fuck buddy, as Michael would say—but something was different now. Something she could feel in her bones.

Later that morning, when the phone rang and it was Poppy, Mona's heart leaped.

Which was ridiculous. Her heart did not leap.

"Good morning, petal."

Even that silly endearment sounded not so silly today.

"Hey there."

"I've got something lovely to show you."

"Oh, yeah?"

"I've printed out a photograph."

"Oh. Some old broad passed out in a creek."

"Stop that. It's beautiful. Can you come by my house this afternoon?"

Mona thought for a moment. "We've got newlyweds arriving, but I'm sure Wilfred and Rhonda can handle it."

"Wonderful. What time?"

"Half an hour?"

"I'll be here."

Mona rushed down the great room where Wilfred and Rhonda were arranging pink peonies that Mr. Hargis had brought in from the garden. "Listen, gang, I've gotta head out for a few hours. Can you hold the fort for me if the newlyweds arrive?

"Sure," said Rhonda.

"Of course," said Wilfred. "Where are you going?"

She decided it was best not to lie. "Just to Poppy's."

"Ah," said Wilfred with the tiniest smirk on his face. "Calligraphy."

She shot him a dagger. "I'll only be gone for a while."

"Take your time," he said. "We got this."

Sometimes she could clobber him.

When Mona arrived at Poppy's millhouse, there was a new bowl of sweet peas on the table in the window. The air smelled of some scent that wasn't the sweet peas, suggesting that Poppy had just sprayed with something floral in preparation.

"I can't wait for you to see this," said Polly. "Would you like some wine first?"

"No, thanks. I have to get back to the guests."

"Well . . . without further ado." She lifted a folder from the table and held it against her chest. "Now this is the one that I like best, but I'm not wedded to it. I want you to be honest with me if you hate it. And if you don't want me to use it at all—"

"Poppy, just show me . . ."

Poppy lowered the folder and opened it to reveal the photo. Mona was momentarily at a loss for words. Far from looking foolish or awkward, the woman in the stream was a Pre-Raphaelite vision come to life. Her expression was peaceful, her mouth slightly open, lingering somewhere between life and death. The ragged bouquet in her hands created bursts of color against the deep green of the surrounding foliage. This wasn't so much Ophelia as Lizzie Siddal's Ophelia come to vivid life.

All Mona could manage was: "You did it."

"Really?"

"It's beautiful, Poppy."

"You're serious?"

"Mmm. Even that stupid prom dress looks good in the water."

"You're not just being nice."

"When am I ever just being nice? You've done it, Poppy. This is magnificent. You're an artist."

Poppy grabbed her and hugged her fiercely. "Please say that again."

Mona chuckled. "You're a fucking artist."

"May I hang it in the post office?"

"Is that the measure of an artist?"

"It is to me."

"Do it, then. I think it's wonderful."

Poppy seized her again and gave her a passionate kiss. Mona returned it for a while, then pulled out of the embrace. "I would love to keep going, but I really do have to get back and be her Ladyship for some guests. Shall we just cuddle for ten minutes?"

"I would love that," said Polly.

So that's what they did on the big green velvet settee over-looking the brook. You could actually hear it from here, Mona realized, and with Poppy's pert breasts pressing into her back, the sound of it was sweeter than ever before.

20

IF YOU KNOW WHAT I MEAN

A decade earlier, when Wilfred and Michael first arrived in the Cotswolds, they were searching for Easley House, without actually knowing it was one of the grandest houses in Gloucestershire. Wilfred had spotted Mona buying a dress in a posh shop in London—her wedding dress, as it turned out—and Michael had wangled the address out of the shop owner. From there, it was a short train ride to Moreton-in-Marsh, where the folks at the Black Bear—Doll and Fred, they were then—told them about a bus tour that would take them directly to Easley House. Doll had died of a heart attack shortly thereafter, and Fred had sold the pub to the current owner and moved to Benidorm.

The subject of the bats came up when he and Rhonda were preparing the bridal bed for the arrival of the newlyweds.

"You're going to think I'm silly."

"Why," she asked, fluffing a pillow. "I thought I heard something last night when I was heading down the hall to the little girls' room."

The infantile expression amused him, but he didn't let on. "What?" he asked.

"Just a sound up above me. It must have been in the attic. Like someone was moving around up there."

"Oh," he smiled broadly. "You've met our other guests."

"I don't understand."

"We have about a dozen bats up there. They roost in the rafters and can be bloody noisy when they're settling in for the night."

Rhonda made a face. "Can't you get rid of them?"

"Why should we? They eat insects and scatter seeds and just want to be left alone. Besides, they're protected. The people from the Bat Society come by once a year to make sure they're okay. We'd get in trouble if they weren't."

"There's a Bat Society?"

"Something like that. Maybe that's just me shorthand."

Rhonda smiled in what looked like relief. "They sure do make a ruckus."

When Mona returned from Poppy's house, Wilfred was still waiting for the guests.

"They shouldn't be long," he told her. "They called from the Black Bear a few minutes ago. They're getting lunch there. Their train was delayed in Oxford."

"Oh, good," said Mona. "We don't have to feed them until dinner."

"They sounded nice," he said.

"What does that mean?"

"They don't sound like Tory twats."

"Well," she said. "That's a start."

When Mona left to check the bridal bedroom, Wilfred spotted some unopened mail on the hall table. He flipped through the pile until he found a letter bearing Michael's unmistakably American handwriting. Normally he would have taken it back to his room for savoring later, but Michael would be arriving in less than a week, and there was no time for leisurely rumination. The letter might contain something he needed to know now.

He tore it open on the window seat and read this:

Dear Wilfred,

Just to let you know, Thack won't be with me when I arrive on the tenth. I'm happy about this because it means that I'll get to have more time with you. I know that this is Mona's show, and I respect that, but please save me some private time.

If you know what I mean.

MICHAEL

Wilfred read the letter three times, trying to make sure he got it right. *What the bloody hell did that mean?* Had the man with whom he'd enjoyed a long-distance platonic friendship for the past ten years just told him that he wanted more than that when he arrived at Easley? Or did he just mean conversation, a chance to hang out privately as friends. That had to be it. It wasn't like Michael to be flirty in a letter. Blokey was as far as it ever went.

On the other hand, if Michael had split from Thack, maybe

he was sending a signal that he was finally available. When Wilfred was sixteen, Michael had kept his distance sexually, but Wilfred was a grown man now, so all bets were off. Unless that was just plain wishful thinking on Wilfred's part. When he was a teenager, he had wanted Michael badly and told him so all the time, but things were different now. The photos he had sent to San Francisco to prove that he was finally a man had elicited sweet compliments but no overtures.

There was no way to know what that letter meant until Wilfred was alone with Michael.

The mere thought of that both excited and terrified him.

He commanded himself to live without expectations for the next five days.

He headed to the greenhouse to harvest a few buds for his room. He often did that before a night in London, just in case he found someone hot with a car and brought him home. Wilfred realized it was scary enough to be led to this house by a stranger, so weed often helped mellow out nervous newcomers. In the back of the greenhouse he found a bud fairly bristling with red hairs and clipped it off with the fold-up pot scissors he kept on his key chain. Michael had given him those scissors five years ago, for his twenty-first birthday, no less, so they were even more rife with meaning at the moment. That's why the voice had frightened him.

"Having a little harvest, are we?"

Wilfred clutched at pearls he almost forgot he had. The man had appeared out of nowhere.

"Don't let me startle you," said Mr. Hargis. He wasn't doffing his cap, but that was his tone of voice. "I can keep a secret, milord."

"It isn't a secret from anybody," Wilfred said, straightening up. "And don't milord me, please. We've had a request for weed from one of the guests."

"Of course."

Why he chose to lie about this was telling. There was no need to lie about pot to Mr. Hargis. He knew everything, and, as caretaker of Easley, was even officially made Guardian of the Greenhouse or some such shit, when Mona realized she needed an accomplice.

Mr. Hargis could keep a secret all right.

So why hadn't Wilfred said it was for his own personal use and left it at that?

Because the moment of its use was already aflame in his head. His big sultan bed where limbs were flailing wildly, and hearts were pumping in sync, and fingers touching places they had never touched before.

And Mr. Hargis really didn't need to be there for that.

21

THAT WOMAN AT THE BOSCOBEL

The newlyweds made virtually no demands on the Easley staff. They barely left the room at all, in fact, so Mona put Wilfred and Rhonda in charge, and headed into Moreton for brunch with Poppy at the Boscobel. The sunny back garden was buzzing with wildflower enthusiasts, who seemed to have arrived en masse by bus.

"They're an interesting lot," said Poppy, as they were sitting down.

"How so?" said Mona.

"Well, they don't seem to know one another at all. It's just wildflowers that brings them together. Or do you suppose they're looking for love as well?"

The garden was mostly middle aged and beyond. Mostly women, too.

"I don't see a lot of possible pairings."

"Don't be so sure. Maybe this is a meet-and-greet for Wildflower Lesbians of the Cotswolds."

Mona chortled into a glass of water. "Then that gentleman over there is in for a rude surprise." She cast her eyes at a chubby bespectacled man sitting by himself next to a trellis of pink roses.

"There has to be someone for him," said Poppy.

"I don't get the sense that he's gay."

"How could you know that?"

"I've had a little practice, petal."

This was the first time Mona had ever thrown that term of endearment back to Poppy.

It wasn't a big deal, but it marked a romantic passage of sorts, and a confession of mutuality.

Poppy gave her a tender smile.

"That woman over there is by herself," said Mona. "Maybe she would work for him."

The subject of their scrutiny was a rather plain horse-faced woman of forty in a long skirt and floral blouse.

Poppy studied him for a moment. "I don't think that would work."

"Why the hell not?"

Poppy shrugged. "I'm pretty sure that's a man."

"What?"

"You know . . . a sex change."

Mona hadn't heard that expression for years. Not to describe a person.

She studied the woman for a moment. "You might be right."

"I know I'm right. But what is he doing on a wildflower tour."

"Maybe looking at wildflowers?"

The irony in Mona's voice was apparently lost on Poppy.

"No . . . I mean, he's not among his own kind here."

"I expect she never is. That's the nature of the beast. You just put on your skirt and some lippy and hope that nobody has the bad manners to address you as he."

"Is that what I'm doing? Showing bad manners?"

"Not yet. But you might stop staring at her, Poppy."

"Fine," said Poppy, looking miffed and picking up a menu. "Let's order."

She knew she should have told Poppy about Anna. Well, she did tell her about a wonderful older friend who used to be her landlady. She just hadn't told her that Anna used to be her father. Now it somehow seemed to be too late. Their sandwiches had arrived, and Mona and Poppy were pecking at them in sullen silence.

Finally Poppy said: "I just don't see what set you off."

"Nothing 'set me off.' You were treating that woman like a freak."

"She didn't hear a word I said."

"That's not the point. I heard it, and . . . I'd like to think you're better than that."

"You can't be serious. What did I say?"

"Just forget it. I'm not going to sit and argue about someone's right to exist. If you can't empathize with——"

"I empathize. He thinks he's one thing . . . excuse me . . . *she* thinks she's one thing, and everyone else can see that she's not. That's just pitiful. I feel sorry for her, Mona. That has to be harder than anything. Living that kind of a lie."

"Maybe she's living her truth."

"No, she's not. Her gender at birth *is* her truth."

Mona didn't want this to go on a moment longer. "Just drop it," she said under her breath, casting a glance at the woman under scrutiny. "She must've heard us. She's leaving."

"There's no way she could have heard us."

They were both looking at her now as she crossed the garden. "She's not leaving," said Mona. "She's just going to the toilet."

Poppy's eyes were filled with panic. "We have to let someone know!"

"That's she's going to the toilet?" Mona gave her a curdled smile. "Oh yes, call out the Royal Marines."

"How can you make light of this, Mona? There could be someone in there already. And what about the other women going in after him?"

Poppy was already rising to leave, so Mona seized her wrist and held tight, speaking in a low authoritative tone. "Sit yourself down, petal. You're not going to make a scene."

A leaden silence fell over them as Mona drove Poppy back to Blockley Brook.

Finally, Mona said: "And just where exactly would you expect her to pee?"

"Well . . . if she must pee—"

"*If she must pee?*"

"—she can slip away quietly to the gents."

"In her paisley skirt and tasteful blouse. That'll work just swell."

"Well, that's *her* problem."

"Why are you so adamant about this?"

"I might ask you the same thing," said Poppy. "I just don't get it. You seem to take it personally."

Mona was in no mood to drag her parent into this debate. Besides, that wasn't the point. "It's just a matter of common decency," she said. "I try to let people be who they are . . . to honor their own version of themselves. It's not that complicated. Think about how hard it is for that woman to go through her day. Do you really want to make it harder?

"That's not fair," said Poppy. "You're making it all about her and her needs. What about the real women who use that toilet? Do you expect them to just deal with the possibility that—" She cut herself off.

"That what? That a dick might be lurking under that paisley."

"Well . . . yes. They don't all have the surgery, do they?"

Mona turned and studied her. "So it's just the presence of a dick that scares you."

"Doesn't it you?"

"Not in and of itself. It's the mind behind the dick, in my experience, and a man striving for womanhood strikes me as the least likely rapist of all."

"In your experience?"

"Are you asking if I know my way around dicks?"

"Yes."

"A bit. There've been a few."

But then again, too few to mention.

"You're bi?"

"I'm Mona . . . but if you wanna call it that . . ."

"Wow," Polly said numbly.

"Trust me, it's not that impressive a roster. And it was a long time ago."

She flashed on that night with Brian Hawkins in the little house on the roof at 28 Barbary Lane, an unexpected moment of carnal tenderness that had grown naturally out of friendship and mutual respect. She had never regretted it, and never wanted more. Which was not to say it couldn't happen again with someone else. She didn't like to make rules for herself.

Noticing the stricken look on Poppy's face, she reached over and squeezed her leg.

"It's all right," she said. "We don't have to be the same."

At Poppy's house they said their goodbyes, both avoiding the prickly issues at hand.

"So when does your masterwork go up?" Mona asked cheerfully, leaning out of the window of her Toyota.

"What do you mean?" asked Poppy.

"The photograph . . . at the post office."

"Oh . . . I have to make a good print first."

"Well, I can't wait to see it."

"You *have* seen it."

"I mean *there* . . . so I can lurk about and receive admirers." It was a lame joke, and she was just trying to lift Poppy's spirits, but it fell flat.

"I'll let you know," said Poppy.

And with that she headed up the path to her house.

All the way back to Easley Mona brooded about Polly's transphobia. There was no other word for it, really. There was fear and disgust in her voice when discussing that woman at the Boscobel. And if she was that afraid of trans people, how could she ever fit into Mona's family? Mona could not begin to love someone like that. She could not begin to love Poppy.

As she pulled into the drive she spotted two young strangers in lawn chairs in front of the house, so she parked the car and strode toward them.

"You must be the Dillards," she said, extending her hand. "I'm Mona Roughton."

"Oh, Lady Roughton," said the woman, shaking her hand, "What a pleasure to meet you!"

"Welcome to Easley House," said Mona. "I hope Wilfred has been taking care of you."

"Yes. And the nice American lady."

Rhonda. The nice American lady.

"I have to tell you," said the woman, slipping her arm around her husband's waist. "We're on our honeymoon, and this is the most wonderful place to be in love."

"That's good to know," said Mona, with only a touch of wistfulness. "Thank you."

She slipped into the house, avoiding the great hall, so as to escape conversation with Wilfred or Rhonda. She didn't want to see anyone right now or, more accurately, didn't want anyone to see her. She would eventually tell Wilfred what had happened, because he would understand, but she couldn't translate this for Rhonda just now. Maybe never. Rhonda had a good heart but was not exactly evolved when it came to understanding difference.

Safely locked in her room, Mona ran a tub with lavender bath salts and had a long soak and a good cry. She had resisted the urge to light a joint, because she knew from experience that pot isn't a remedy for grief. If anything it amplifies it. And grief was exactly what she was feeling, because the long-awaited possibility of love had just died a swift and terrible death.

22

A FAILURE OF THE HEART

Midsummer's Eve was on June 21, just three days after Michael was slated to arrive at Easley House. Wilfred knew there was work to be done right away if they were to have a proper pagan celebration. That meant pies to be baked and ivy to be gathered for garlands and firewood to be stacked for the bonfire, not to mention an abundant supply of scrumpy and weed. Normally, Mona would be on this like a demon, but she had been oddly listless for several days. He knew better than to ask her why. She would share her woes in her own time.

The bonfire was always built in a clearing at the far end of the estate, where it could leap high into the night sky without spreading to nearby trees or endangering man or beast. There was a permanent circle of ashes there that betrayed the ceremonial purpose of that space. Even off-season Wilfred loved it, because it conjured up the fire rituals of his Aboriginal ancestors, rituals as old as Dreamtime, and far older, of course, than Merrie Olde England itself.

The firewood had to be brought in. For many years they had used the remains of a fallen cedar that burned nicely and left an aromatic tang in the air. But last year they had been forced to import kiln-dried oak from a firm in Stow. Mr. Hargis had arranged it and supervised the stacking in the fire circle. It was time to do that again.

He wandered the grounds in search of the old man. Finally, after checking the greenhouse and the rose beds, he spotted Mr. Hargis coming out of the chapel. There was no religious reason for the chapel anymore, ever since Mona and Lord Teddy were married there, so Mr. Hargis used it for storing lawn mowers and other garden equipment. He called out the gardener's name but there was no response. His hearing was getting worse, Wilfred realized.

Moving closer to the chapel, he called again. This time Mr. Hargis jerked his head around, seemingly startled.

"Oh, Lord Wilfred."

There was no point in correcting him anymore. The old man was seriously wedded to the old ways.

"I've been meaning to talk to you about Midsummer's Eve."

"Oh yes?"

"It's coming up in a few days, and we'll need lots of firewood for the bonfire. I seem to remember you getting it from a place in Stow."

"Oh yes. Ol' Dalrymple and his lads."

The lads were the important detail here, since they did all the heavy lifting and the actual construction of the bonfire.

"Good, good," said Wilfred. "Do you want me to call them?"

"No, milord. I can call them from my house when I go back for lunch."

Mr. Hargis's "house" was just outside the gate, an upstairs bedroom in the home of a local widow, who apparently cooked for him and did his laundry. He had lived there ever since his beloved Elspeth had died. Whether it went any further than that was anyone's guess, but it was clear that he needed the presence of a woman to make it through life.

"Oh," said Wilfred, remembering, "and we'll need lots of ivy and cut flowers for wreaths."

"Yes, milord, the usual."

This made him wonder about something. "Did Lord Teddy's father observe Midsummer's Eve?"

"Oh, no milord, he was a devout Christian."

Mr. Hargis cast an anxious glance back at the chapel as the Jesus in the stained glass might strike him down for helping with a pagan celebration.

"You know it's just silly fun for me and Lady Mona?"

The old man just nodded absently and began to walk away from the chapel. "Ivy, roses, and firewood," he muttered, as if compiling a checklist.

Poor ol' geezer, thought Wilfred. He's really beginning to lose it.

W ilfred found Mona in the kitchen furiously chopping apples for pies. He held back in the doorway for a moment, observing the process.

"What?" she said, finally noticing him.

"You're murdering that fruit," he said.

"Mind your own business."

"Something's bugging you. What is it?"

"Nothing's bugging me," she snapped, still chopping away. "Michael is arriving in a matter of days, and I don't want to waste that time cooking. We have to prepare in advance. This house doesn't run itself, you know."

The implication that he wasn't pulling his share of the load annoyed the hell out of him. "I just arranged for the bonfire. And flowers and ivy for the wreaths. I'm just as excited about seeing Michael as you are."

"I know," she said in a much softer tone.

He reached out and seized one of her hands, holding it until she looked up with Princess Diana puppy-dog eyes. She only resorted to that when she wanted sympathy.

"Is this about Poppy?"

Her shrug meant yes.

"Did she dump you?"

"No. If anything, I'm about to dump her."

"Why?"

"She has some truly fucked-up views about trans people."

"Oh . . . you told her about Anna?"

"No. There was a trans woman having lunch at the Boscobel. Just another customer at the next table. It set her off like you wouldn't believe. She practically tackled the poor thing on the way to the ladies' room."

"Oh, dear . . ."

"You can say that again."

"So you've *never* told her about Anna." It wasn't a question; it was a realization.

"What does that have to do with anything?"

"I'm just curious as to why you never said anything in . . . what? . . . five years?"

"It hasn't been serious until very recently."

Wilfred nodded, taking that in. "Just a good shag and a handy calligrapher."

"Pretty much. Yeah."

"Why spoil a good thing, right?"

"Are you judging me?"

"No . . . but you might have educated her, Mo. Whether you were serious or not."

"This isn't a failure of education, Wilfred. It's a failure of the heart. I can't build a life around someone so utterly lacking in empathy. And if I had told her about Anna, I might not have seen this side of her at all. I've always thought she was a little tight-assed for an artist, but this was the deal-breaker."

There was nothing left to do but sympathize. "I'm really sorry, Mo."

"I knew you'd get it," she said. "I raised you right."

"Are you sad?"

"Oh, hell yeah."

"What can I do to help?"

She thought for a moment. "You could make a nice flower arrangement for Michael's room to welcome him here."

"Easy. We've got masses of pansies right now."

She smiled. "Isn't that a little on the nose?"

"Not for him. He'll love it."

"All right, then . . . but Wilfred . . ."

"Yes?"

"Just because Thack isn't coming with him doesn't mean you should . . . have expectations."

"I know that. C'mon, Mo, gimme some credit. This ain't my first time at the rodeo."

"I just don't want you getting hurt. I've seen him break a few hearts in my time."

He wondered what she meant by that but decided not to pursue it. "I'm a grown man, Mo. I can take care of meself."

That wasn't exactly the truth, but it would have to do for now.

23

THE WILD CARD

Thack had left Michael's life as suddenly as he had appeared. They first laid eyes on each other in a darkened cell at Alcatraz, surrounded by a dozen Catholic schoolgirls on a tour of the prison. It had made them both grin and swap knowing glances when the lights came up, and they were off and running after that, giddy with the discovery of new love.

The end had come just as suddenly. One morning about a month ago Thack left for a friend's house in the Mission on a motorcycle he had bought with their joint Mastercard. They would talk later, he said. He needed space, he said, meaning any space without you in it. Michael had needed that, too, he realized. Thack's volcanic temper was exhausting him.

Easley House would be the perfect break—some quality time with Mona and Wilfred in that magnificent old house in the Cotswolds. And Anna, of course, who would be seeing the house for the first time. There was even a Midsummer ritual planned, whatever that meant.

It was Wilfred who mostly occupied Michael's thoughts as he packed for the trip. Wilfred was the wild card here. Michael knew what he looked like, because he was still sending photos, but that rangy man in the recent snapshots was a far cry from the impish youth Michael had met at the Coleherne a decade earlier. He had even bulked up noticeably since their reunion in London five years ago. And all the letters they had swapped over the years were no substitute for an in-person conversation. Letters only told you what people wanted you to know. It was best not to have expectations of any kind.

24

HOLDING THE FORT

Rhonda had inaugurated a thorough cleaning of Easley House prior to the arrival of Mona and Wilfred's friend from San Francisco. It was obvious that this man mattered a great deal to them both, so that became the inspiration for their labors. The great hall was sparkling like a diamond when they were finished, and everyone seemed to draw satisfaction from it.

"Wow," said Wilfred, leaning on his mop, "this place hasn't looked this good since you were married."

"I know," said Mona, "and we have Rhonda to thank for it."

"Pshaw," said Rhonda.

"Pshaw?" said Wilfred with a quizzical look.

"Just something my mama used to say when you paid her a compliment."

"Well, I meant it," said Mona. "You got our asses in gear."

"I hope I wasn't too bossy."

Wilfred smiled at her. "It was just the right amount."

"And now," said Mona, discarding her dustrag with a flourish,

"I think we should drive into Cheltenham for the summer crafts festival. We got some great shit there last year, and I wouldn't mind having another ramble through the stalls before Michael gets here. We can have lunch there, too. There's lots of good food. We owe it to ourselves."

Mona was looking at Rhonda as she said this. "You mean me as well?" asked Rhonda.

"Of course you as well."

"And leave the house unattended?"

"What's gonna happen? It's been here for eight hundred years. It won't mind if we play hooky for an afternoon."

"What happens if someone drops by?"

"Well, they can just drop the fuck away again."

Rhonda seemed to ponder something. "You know what? Let me stay and hold the fort. I really don't mind. In fact, I think I'd enjoy it."

"Oh, c'mon," said Wilfred.

"I mean it," said Rhonda. "It would be fun. I can pretend I'm lady of the manor."

Mona stared at her in disbelief. "You know," she said, turning to Wilfred, "I think she actually means it."

"Sure. I can cuddle on the couch with Nilla and read a book and make myself a nice pot of tea. I could use the downtime."

Mona made a last feeble effort. "The crafts festival is really a lot of fun."

"I'm sure it is. Bring me a pot holder."

Mona gave her a sideways glance. "Are you taking the piss?"

"*Doing what?*"

"It's just an English expression. It means . . . never mind."

She sent them on their way from the drive, watching as the old green Toyota passed through the gatehouse and out of sight. Standing near the gatehouse, Mr. Hargis gave them a wave and a tip of his hat. He seemed to be everywhere and nowhere, that old man, but Rhonda drew some comfort from knowing that she would not be completely alone at Easley.

She went back into the house and made herself a pot of tea in the kitchen. It was completely her choice as to where she would take it, so she settled after some deliberation on the library. She had always liked the atmosphere of that cozy old room, with its floor-to-ceiling books and dark paneling. There was an especially comfy-looking wingback chair in one corner, so she settled there and poured herself a cup of tea.

It amazed her how natural it felt to be here. She had been joking when she said she could be lady of the manor for a day, but it did feel like that now as she breathed in the scents and sounds of the old house. There was nothing this old back in North Carolina, nothing with this much serious antiquity seeping from its bones. Even the noises it made from time to time seemed to be calling from another century. But that whisper from the doorway that had startled her a moment ago had proved to be nothing more that Nilla, cruising for a chin scratch from the last remaining resident. Rhonda obliged her while the dog crooned.

She supposed that lots of folks, Americans especially, would be spooked by a house like this, but not Rhonda. She found comfort in Easley, a curious sort of reassurance that what was past was permanently past. If bad things had happened here over the centuries, there was nothing left of those grim episodes now. Easley felt more like something out of Agatha Christie, cozy and goose bumpy but nothing to be seriously worried about.

That gave her an idea. She went to the great wall of books behind her and searched for anything by Agatha Christie. She found a novel called *The Mysterious Affair at Styles*, with a manor house on the cover that looked a lot like Easley. It would be the perfect book for curling up in the window seat in the great hall. She had seen Wilfred do that, and it looked like fun.

She was there in the window seat when she saw a figure running across the lawn and darting into the woods. His back was turned to her, but it clearly wasn't Mr. Hargis, since he moved too fast for that. Was this the Old Gypsy that Mr. Hargis talked about chasing from the estate? Had he come back because he knew the car was gone and the house might be empty? Would she be forced to confront him? The thought of that was completely daunting. She could handle anyone who rang the bell, but this was ominously different.

She went up to her room and locked the door. She could see the lawn clearly from her window, and the intruder was nowhere in sight.

For the rest of the afternoon she read in her room until the others returned.

25

SLEEPING ARRANGEMENTS

Michael ate a Cadbury fruit bar in the Oxford train station as he waited for Anna to return from the ladies' room. She emerged in a blur of summery green silk, an outfit that had served her well yesterday on the airplane (even when she was sleeping), and promised to do the same this afternoon at an English manor house. That was the very essence of Anna, he thought: she might wear the clothes, but they never wore her. She had style in the Quentin Crisp sense of the word and knew that it wasn't remotely the same as being fashionable.

"That looks good," she said, eyeing his Cadbury bar.

"Want one of your own?"

"Oh, no . . . well, maybe just a smidgen. She mimed that amount with her thumb and forefinger. Michael broke off a small chunk and handed it to her. She sat down next to him and chewed delicately while murmuring her appreciation.

"You know," she said, "I read somewhere that English ladies

always carry a stash of chocolate in their purse so they never find themselves without it. I don't know if that's true, but it makes complete sense to me. Chocolate is good for emergencies."

Michael smiled at her. "You aren't having one now, are you?"

"An emergency? Not at all. I *am* glad we didn't come directly from the plane. I'm feeling fresh as a daisy after ten hours of sleep."

It had taken Michael at least ten days to recover from jet lag when he flew from San Francisco to London in the early eighties. And every day of that time he had woken at 3 a.m. filled with restless anxiety and unable to go back to sleep for hours. Leave it to this hardy septuagenarian to be fully recovered after a good night's sleep at an airport Best Western.

"You amaze me," he said.

She shrugged. "I've always slept like a baby. Shall we buy sandwiches for this last leg of the journey?"

"Good idea. We don't want to arrive famished."

They bought egg and cress sandwiches and ate them on the train as the green English countryside unrolled before them. There were long silences during which Anna would gaze out the window, seemingly lost in her thoughts.

"You know," she said at last, "this isn't the first time I've tracked her down."

"What do you mean?"

"Just that . . . I had to arrange to meet her before she moved into Barbary Lane. I knew she was my daughter, but she had no idea that I was her father."

"l remember," he said quietly.

"It was such a risk, really. She might have fled in horror, or told me off for being such a terrible parent."

"That would never have happened."

Anna turned and looked at him. "But it could have, dear. It could have very easily. I deserted her and her mother when I left Minneapolis, and I never once looked back. I didn't deserve to get a second chance."

"But thank heavens you did, because I wouldn't have known you. It was Mona, remember, who brought me to Barbary Lane."

"That's right," she said softly, as if realizing this for the first time.

"Do I detect a little soul-searching?"

"Maybe a little."

"Well, stop it, woman. You're the best old broad I know."

She made a little grunt that said she doubted that.

"And," he added, changing the subject, "you're going to flip when you see this house. No photograph can do it justice."

"You still haven't told her I'm coming with you?"

"Nope. It would rob her of a wonderful surprise."

Their driver, a bald man with dramatic eyebrows, leaned over the seat to address them.

"You must be Lady Mona's American family."

Anna was noticeably pleased. "We are," she said. "She's my daughter."

"I thought so! She's the spittin' image of her mum."

Anna hesitated then murmured a subdued "Thank you." Michael caught her eye with a sly smile. "Everybody says that," he told the driver.

When Easley House came into view across a broad expanse of lawn, Anna uttered a little gasp. "That can't be it," she said.

"Why can't it?"

"It's just so . . . majestic."

"And you were worried she wouldn't have room for you."

"Well, I know she takes in guests."

"Not this week. We'll have the whole joint to ourselves."

The driver tapped on his horn as they approached the house. Not the most elegant of entrances, Michael thought, but then again this was Mona, and she and the driver must have long ago established the protocol of these taxi runs from the Black Bear.

Moments later, the lady of the manor came charging out of the nondescript door and cavorting like a madwoman as he emerged from the cab.

"Oh Mouse," she screamed. "Oh Mouse."

He thought for a moment she was going to jump and wrap her legs around his waist like she did in the old days, but knowing that neither one of them was likely to survive it, she went for a bear hug instead. They just stood there rocking and crooning in the warm June sunshine, until she recognized the other occupant of the cab.

"Holy fucking shit!"

She fell to her knees by the door. "It's a goddamn miracle!"

A stony face framed in silver hair scolded quietly from within the cab. "You're making a scene, dear. Must there always be drama?"

"Hell, yeah," said Mona. "I think there must."

Still on her knees, she turned her head to speak to Michael. "Were you behind this, you sneaky bastard?"

"We were both behind it . . . two sneaky bastards." He was grinning, very pleased with himself. Anna was smiling, too. "Now let me get out."

Mona rose and opened the door for her.

"Welcome to Easley, Your Majesty."

Anna was a little wobbly as she left the cab. "Don't call me that again," she said, steadying herself. "I might get used to it. Where is my grandchild?"

"He's coming," said Mona, just as Wilfred came bursting out of the door. How he loves making an entrance, she thought. "Wilfred Porter, meet your grandmother, Anna Madrigal."

Wilfred stepped forward, clicked his heels, and gave her a jaunty salute. Anna beckoned him for a hug, which he readily accepted. "Goodness, you've grown."

"Hasn't he?" said Michael, standing nearby and observing the two of them.

Wilfred turned and smiled at Michael. "Hey, mate," he said quietly. To Michael, it was an extraordinarily intimate moment, as if they were the only two people around.

Michael stepped forward and gave him a brief hug, ending with a pat on the back. Anything more than that—if anything more was in the cards—would have to wait until they were alone. There were too many witnesses at the moment.

As Mona led them into the great hall the place struck Michael as a remembered dream. He had been here before, of course, but he had almost stopped believing in the reality of those honey-colored stained-glass windows, this cavernous fireplace, the minstrels' gallery high above them where he had first spotted Mona a decade earlier. Anna paid it all the reverence of silence as she stood in the middle of the room, eyes lifted and mouth agape, soaking it in. "Well," she said at last, "we've come a long way from the Blue Moon Lodge."

Mona laughed and took Anna's arm. "I'm so glad you're here."

A woman Michael didn't recognize emerged from the kitchen and set a tray of canapés on the long table in the center of the room. "I thought you folks might like some nibbles after your journey." Her accent was readily identifiable as American Southern.

"Oh, Rhonda," said Mona, "these are my friends, Anna and Michael. Rhonda's a friend who's been staying with us for a while, and she's the best cook in the house."

Michael surveyed the contents of the tray. "Those look an awful lot like bourbon balls."

"They *are* bourbon balls!" Rhonda's face was aglow with pride.

Michael put a fist on his hip. "Where are you from, girl?"

Rhonda looked slightly taken aback. "North Carolina."

"I'm from Florida," said Michael. "I grew up on bourbon balls." He plucked one of the powdered sugar balls off the tray and popped it into his mouth.

"Where the hell did you get the bourbon?" asked Mona.

"In the village," said Rhonda. "Mrs. O'Leary in the liquor shop ordered me a bottle."

Mona shook her head with a dim smile. "Well, you are just *full* of surprises."

"What else is in it?" asked Anna, reaching for a bourbon ball.

"Well, just toasted pecans and powdered sugar and vanilla wafers."

"Speaking of which," said Mona, as Nilla emerged from the kitchen to investigate the visitors. "This is Miss Vanilla Wafer."

The dog wove her way around Michael and Anna with her tail flying like a banner.

"Well, look at you," said Michael. "Where did you come from?"

"I inherited her from a friend, who couldn't care for her anymore," Mona told him.

"Why not?"

Mona hesitated, so Rhonda jumped in. "He was dying of AIDS."

"Oh," said Michael. "Silly me. What else?" He exchanged a rueful glance with Mona, who shrugged in acknowledgment. "Can't get away from it, can you?"

Rhonda touched her hand to her chest. "I hope I didn't speak out of turn."

"Not at all," said Mona. "We're all family here."

Mona took Anna upstairs to see her room. Wilfred and Michael followed shortly thereafter.

"Anna's getting the fancier room," Wilfred explained, as he carried Michael's suitcase. "We didn't know she was coming, but . . . Mona felt she should have the one we prepared."

"Say no more," said Michael. "I agree completely."

"Yours is nice, too."

"They all look nice to me."

Wilfred chuckled. "Believe me, some of them are a little scary."

"I'm so glad I'm here," said Michael.

Wilfred touched him on the arm. "Same here, bud." Michael wondered if something more was about to happen, but Wilfred just turned and opened a door.

"Wa-la!"

The room seemed fine to Michael. A comfy-looking single bed, a couple of faded velvet armchairs, a view of the green hills beyond. He did wonder if the single bed was meant to signal his sleeping arrangements for the stay, but then he remembered that the "nicer room" had previously been intended for him. "Where do you sleep?" he asked Wilfred.

"At the end of the hall . . . under the eaves."

"Sounds terribly . . . exotic." He was going to say romantic, but the word was just too loaded.

"I'll show it to you later. If you like. Meanwhile . . ." He set down Michael's suitcase. "I know you want to settle in. This room has its own sink and shower, and there's a superb bathtub in Anna's room that I'm sure she would let you use."

"I'm fine," said Michael, sitting on the edge of the bed as if to prove it.

"Just come down to the great hall when you've freshened up. I'll give you me tour of the house and grounds."

Michael smiled at him wanly. "I've been here before, re-member?"

"Yeah but . . . that was a long time ago."

It *was* a long time ago, thought Michael. The flirty boy who tried like hell to seduce him was taller now—taller than Michael, in fact—and exuded a kind of gravitas that bordered on intimidating. All those letters over the years had done nothing to signal the man Wilfred was to become. Just as much as the old house itself, Wilfred would require re-education.

He thought it best not to remark on the past. "By the way," he said, "is that nice Southern lady Mona's latest?"

Wilfred shook his head vehemently. "She initially came as a guest and has stayed as a friend."

Michael arched an eyebrow in suspicion. "I dunno. Sounds an awful lot like the way Mona operates."

Wilfred widened his eyes. "I don't think they're doing it, if that's what you mean."

"Just a friend," said Michael. "Got it."

"Rhonda's husband beat the shit out her one too many times while they were staying here, so . . . we helped her escape . . . and she stayed on."

"Where is the husband then?"

Wilfred shrugged. "Beats me. Back in Tarbilly, I guess."

"Where?"

"Somewhere in North Carolina. Him and me didn't get on. He called me a stuck-up British pickaninny."

He cracked a smile, so Michael followed suit. "Well, that's original, as racism goes."

"Yeah, but only me mates get to call me that."

Michael laughed. Here, briefly, was the Wilfred he remembered.

M ona and Wilfred led a house tour after Anna and Michael had freshened up. Leading them down a hallway lined with stern old portraits, Wilfred turned to Mona and said: "Now spare us the fabrications, milady."

Mona scowled at him.

"She makes up stories about these people," Wilfred explained. "For the amusement of the visitors."

"Well, look at them," said Mona, indicating the blackened portrait of a dour woman with a doily on her head. "No one knows who the fuck she is, so there might as well be a story. And what's wrong with being called a Sapphic mystic? That's much more interesting than what she probably was. I'm doing her a favor really. What's going on with that hat?"

At the end of the hallway, Wilfred opened a door that led to a small outdoor space, very high up. "What's this? The parapet?" asked Michael.

"More or less," said Wilfred. "It's the best view around. Over there's the folly. You remember that, don't you, Michael?"

"Oh, yeah." Michael appreciated this little nod to their shared past.

"This is just marvelous," said Anna, taking it all in. "What's that little building down there?"

"Oh, that's the chapel," said Mona. "That's where Teddy and I were married. Haven't been back since." She punctuated that remark with a tiny curdled smile.

"You have your own chapel. That's amazing," said Anna.

"It isn't very useful nowadays. Mr. Hargis uses it to store his lawnmower."

"Who's Mr. Hargis?

"The gardener."

"I remember him," said Michael.

Mona tried to elaborate: "I'm afraid he's out of it these days. He chases imaginary Gypsies and comes and goes as he pleases. He's been here since Teddy was born, so I don't have the heart to let him go. Besides, he loves Easley and he still mows the lawn."

"I understand," said Anna quietly. "You're being kind."

Mona shrugged off the compliment. Praise had always made her squirm, Michael realized.

"And over yonder," said Wilfred, pointing to the left, "is the bluebell wood. They were lovely this year, but I'm afraid they were gone by May. They come back every year to that woodland and some folks reckon they've done that for the past three hundred years."

"Really?" said Anna in amazement. "How do you know such things?"

"By living here. Easley's a great teacher. She taught me everything I know."

"So it's a she?" said Michael.

"She is now," said Mona. "Mama don't allow no patriarchy round here."

Both visitors laughed. "Well, some things never change," said Michael.

Wilfred and Mona led the way back into the house. Michael followed with Anna, holding tight to her arm on the tricky stairs.

"You can bust your ass on these things."

"No different from Barbary Lane," said Anna.

When they finally reached the great hall, there was tea laid out on the big table, obviously the work of the Southern woman they had met on the way in.

"Aren't you a dear?" said Anna, accepting a finger sandwich from her.

Michael was once again glad he'd insisted on Anna coming along. She compounded the pleasure for him, the melding of old memories and new discoveries.

26

COMPLETE STRANGERS

Anna knew that Michael and Mona needed time to catch up, so she left them in the library, and set off on a leisurely stroll through the garden. The morning was toasty warm and melodious with birds. The sky was as every bit as deep blue as a Northern California sky. She felt a curious contentment in this exotic place, as if she had always been meant to be here.

Ten minutes into her walk she was joined by the big yellow dog she had met yesterday.

"Why good morning, Miss Nilla. How are you, this fine day?"

The dog kissed her hand lavishly and encircled her twice.

"Would you like to join me on my walk?"

Nilla seemed to understand, or at least to understand the universal w-word, because her tail started wagging furiously.

"All right, then," said Anna. "Lead the way."

Nilla did just that, running ahead of Anna through the woodland, circling back to let the old lady catch up.

"Are we going somewhere?" asked Anna.

The dog barked twice in response and headed into a dense stand of trees that seemed to conceal a small building. Anna recognized it immediately, though she hadn't seen it from this angle before. She had seen it from the roof of the house, when Wilfred was pointing out the sites of interest. This was the chapel where Mona and Lord Teddy were married.

Nilla ran to the door and pawed it politely. When no response came she turned and looked at Anna expectantly.

"I don't think we should," said Anna, upon which a voice in her head said: *Why not? The lady of the manor is your daughter, and you've come all this way. Why not see the place where she was married. She couldn't possibly mind.*

She stepped forward and turned the doorknob. The door opened with a rusty creak, and Nilla rushed past her into the chapel.

Then came a voice from inside: "Hello there, sweet girl, who've you brought with you?" For a moment, she couldn't see the source of the voice, until a man reclining on one of the pews lifted his head into view.

"I'm terribly sorry," said Anna. "I thought it was empty. I'm . . . a guest at the house, and this place peaked my curiosity."

"More like Nilla's curiosity," said the man. "She likes to visit me here." He rose to a seated position and cradled the dog's head in his hand. His face was careworn and unshaven, his clothes wrinkled and dusty.

Anna knew that this must be the gardener who was, in Mona's words, "losing it." As further proof, his riding lawn mower and several muddy rakes were visible nearby.

"I'm so sorry to disturb you," she said.

"No, no. I was just having a little snooze." He gestured to-ward a chair next to the pew.

"Please. Sit down. I could use the company."

She could see the truth of this in his eyes, so she obeyed. "It's a lovely little chapel, isn't it?" She gazed up at a stained-glass Jesus holding a baby lamb in his arms.

"It's not really a chapel anymore," he said. "but it makes me feel peaceful."

"I can see that," she murmured.

"I lost my wife recently, and . . . I still can't stop thinking about all the things I should've said to her."

Anna smiled dimly. "We humans tend to do that, don't we?"

He just sat there, head dangling between his knees, but he seemed to agree.

"I'm sorry about your wife."

"Thank you."

"How long did you have together?"

"Thirty-four years."

"Long time."

He nodded. "Not long enough, though."

"You know," said Anna, reaching for one of his hands, "you can still talk to her. She's there for you if you need her."

He just shook his head slowly. "I don't think so."

She squeezed his hand. "Why not just try it? Just list the things you want to say to her. You will feel so much better, I promise. You'll have closure."

The man said nothing, but a thought seemed to be forming in his head. "I guess I've still been afraid of facing her."

"Don't do that. Don't be afraid. You've nothing at all to lose."

"You know," said the man, after a moment's pondering, "you really make a lot of sense."

Anna smiled at him and let go of his hand. "That's not like me at all. I must be having an off day."

She rose from the pew and dusted off her skirt. "Meanwhile, kind sir . . . I must get back to my walk."

Nilla heard the w-word and rose from the mat where she had settled herself. They left the chapel together and went on their way.

She got lost for a while in a green woodland that she assumed was the famous bluebell wood, well past its glory days. Finding a bench near the center, she sat down. It was a lovely place to contemplate the miracle of chance encounters, the intimacy that could sometimes happen between complete strangers. She had left that old gardener with a glimmer of hope in his heart, and even if they were never to meet again, that was worth everything to her.

27

A LITTLE TRUE

Mona and Michael were hanging out in the library, both curled up in well-worn armchairs.

"How many have you lost?" asked Michael.

Mona shrugged. "Do we have to keep count, Mouse?

"Sorry. I've stopped doing that, too."

"Nilla's dad was the big one last year. And a caterer I knew, and six months later, his boyfriend. And lots of men Wilfred knew in the village, some of whom were still students. A plumber I'd worked with. An old professor who never talked about it. Make me stop."

"Stop," said Michael softly.

"Most of the ones I knew were gorgeous. What is that all about? Do they just get more sex *because* they're gorgeous, or did they hang out in the same bars, or what? And don't tell me the angel of death is punishing them for being pretty."

Michael smiled at her. "Your whole premise is faulty. I know plenty of ugly guys who died of AIDS."

Mona recoiled in shock. "Mouse."

"Well, I do. I did. Nobody's escaping."

"I know. I guess we only notice the pretty ones who get it. Wilfred knows three Love Muscle dancers who died of it."

"What the fuck is a Love Muscle dancer?"

"Just these guys at a club in Brixton. Bodybuilders who flop out their dicks onstage at closing time."

"Have you been there?"

"Oh hell no. I've seen enough of those to last me a lifetime."

Michael chuckled. "Never going back to dicks, huh."

"I didn't say that. I'm not going anywhere right now."

"What about that postmistress?"

"What about her?"

"Is that still a thing?"

"No longer. Great in the sack, but she turned out to be a raging transphobe."

"Oh no. You told her about Anna?"

"No. But she made it really clear how she felt about our sisters. I just can't have that, Mouse. Sure, she needs to evolve . . . everybody needs to . . . but she can do it on her own time. For me, life's just too damn short."

"I hear you."

"And please don't mention this to Anna.

"Why?"

"Because she'll blame herself for it, and end up trying to fix things. That would be horrific. Just don't, okay."

Michael crossed his heart. She obviously meant it.

"Have you talked to Wilfred yet? I mean alone."

Leave it to Mona to shift the focus back to him. "Sure, but . . .

it was kind of formal. It felt as if he were checking me into a hotel."

"Whatcha think we've been doing here, buster?"

"Sure, but . . . maybe he was just scared. I certainly was."

"You? What have you got to be scared of? You've swapped letters with Wilfred for years."

"That's just it. He feels deeply familiar now. Like my little brother. And do I really want to—"

"Stop right there. Don't finish that."

"Good. You catch my drift. It all gets a little incestuous, doesn't it? He's your son, after all! I can't just bag him."

"What makes you think that's up to you?"

"C'mon. I didn't mean it like that. I'm well aware that I might not be . . . of interest to him."

"And I'm well aware that you and Thack are on the rocks, and I don't want my son to be your rebound adventure."

"That's a little harsh."

"It's a little true."

"He's twenty-six years old, Mona."

"And you're . . . you're . . . what? Forty-five? . . . But you're just as needy as ever. You're lethal when you're needy, Mouse. We both know that."

A troubling thought occurred to him. "Did Wilfred tell you to say this to me?"

"Of course not! This is just me."

"Then kindly change the subject." He softened his tone for the rest. "And don't worry. We're pretty much on the same page."

"I'm not on any page. I just love both of you. And I don't want anybody hurt."

"I get it," he said.

"Shall we have a picnic on the lawn this evening?"

He smiled at her. "Yes, please."

"I've grown some killer weed. Do you still enjoy that?"

"I was waiting for you to ask."

"Does Anna?"

"Are you kidding? Some things never change. But we promised each other we wouldn't travel with it."

"Good. They're awful about it here. You have to be careful when you're traveling."

"Is the picnic part of the Midsummer festivities?"

"No. That's a few days down the line. There's a big bonfire and we make wishes as we march around it."

"Oh dear."

"Don't worry, it's fun. And the wishes have to be private."

"Is this part the pagan stuff?"

"Technically it's St. John's Day. The Vatican hijacked it from the pagans in the fourth century. That's why there are bonfires and maypoles."

"You have a *maypole*?"

"Hell no. That's much too phallic for me. I ain't dancin' around no dick. They do that at the Anglican church during the bake sale."

Michael laughed.

"It's a funny old country," she said.

"It seems to agree with you."

"Oh yes. In ways that I haven't even discovered yet."

He could tell that she meant that.

"Do me a favor," she said after a while. "Don't mention the pagan thing to Rhonda."

"Who's Rhonda?"

"The bourbon balls lady. She's Christian, and I don't want her to freak out."

Michael widened his eyes at her. "That's not like you at all."

"I know, but I like her. And she's basically kind, and she's been through holy hell with an asswipe of a husband."

"Yeah, Wilfred told me."

"He was a monster. He'd been beating her up for years."

"How did you get rid of him?"

"We made him think she'd gone back to London, so he went looking for her."

"And she's been with you ever since?'

"Yep. And she's been a helpful addition to the household."

"I can see that," said Michael. "She can cook, for one thing."

Mona narrowed her eyes at him. "Don't be a smartass. I'm a lot better than I used to be."

28

A GRACIOUS PLENTY

Wilfred and Rhonda were in the kitchen, preparing fried chicken for the picnic.

"I was surprised to find buttermilk in the village," said Rhonda.

"Is that for the batter?" asked Wilfred.

"Eventually, yes. But first we soak the chicken in it. There are enzymes in it that tenderize the chicken better than anything else."

Wilfred watched as she dunked chicken pieces into a large ceramic bowl of buttermilk. "Who knew?" he said, adding several more pieces himself. "Now what?"

"We let it soak for an hour or so. I usually like to do it overnight, but this will be a gracious plenty."

"A what?"

"A gracious plenty. We say that in the South. It means . . . I dunno . . . just the right amount."

"No kidding."

"I guess I sound quaint to you."

"Not at all. I think you're lovely."

Rhonda blushed vividly.

"I mean, you know . . . your accent."

"Thank you. I like your accent, too."

Wilfred rolled his eyes. "It's not very posh."

"What does that mean?"

"I dunno. Snooty. Upper class."

"Oh, well, I'm not very posh either. Ernie used to tell me I sounded like a hick. Like a damn Cherokee."

"I thought we told that bellend to sod off."

"I guess I won't ask what that means." She smiled at him faintly.

"You catch me drift, anyway."

"The thing is," Rhonda went on, "I'm glad we're not in the same country anymore, I really am. But it all happened so quick. I never really got to have my say."

"Well, we had to act quickly or—"

"Oh, I don't mean you and Mona did anything wrong. You did everything right, in fact. I'm just still so angry at Ernie . . . and I never got to tell him off."

Wilfred placed a drumstick into the buttermilk. "Then what would you have said to him?

Rhonda thought for a moment. "So many things, really. How I spent my whole life apologizing to him, when it should have been the other way around."

"Check."

"And . . . that he always put me down in front of his friends."

"I know that one. That was popular with several of me boyfriends."

That threw her for a moment. Then she said: "Have you had many? Boyfriends, I mean?"

"Not many. It's harder for a queer lad living in the country."

"Really?"

"I know, you'd think it wouldn't be in such a pretty place. But they're all either closeted or holed up in their houses with some other bloke. I have to take the train to meet somebody nice, and even then I don't make it to the boyfriend stage very often."

"That's too bad."

Wilfred shrugged. "There are worse things. Like not living here or . . . having someone like Ernie."

Rhonda remained silent.

"You deserved so much better than him, Rhonda. You're pretty and kind . . . and you can cook like an angel."

"Hush now."

"I love when you say . . . 'hush now.' It's an order, but it sounds like a lullaby."

She didn't look up from soaking a chicken breast. "Then obey it, please. I'm not comfortable with compliments."

"Wooo . . ."

"Anyway, we were talking about you."

"Oh, yes. Where were we? Oh . . . you were wishing I could find a boyfriend. Now tell me, is that any way to be a good Christian?"

"You are so bad."

"I know."

"Just because I love Jesus doesn't mean I can't love you, too."

It surprised him how much this embarrassed him.

———

They added paprika to the chicken, deep-fried it, and drained it. Then they boiled half a dozen cobs of corn, and began to pack the gargantuan Fortnum & Mason hamper.

"Would our guests like some scrumpy?" asked Rhonda.

Wilfred raised an eyebrow and smiled. "I've already got a gracious plenty in the fridge."

"Good."

"You like that stuff, don't you?"

Rhonda gave him a scolding look, then changed the subject. "This picnic basket is magnificent. I love the lining."

"It was a present," said Wilfred. "We could never afford something like this. It was packed with wine and biscuits and cakes."

"What a nice friend!"

"Well, that's just it. She isn't a friend at all. She just sends things from time to time because she wants us to sell her this house."

"Who is she?"

"Her name is Fabia Dane. Her husband made a fortune selling crisps. She knows we're skint and figures we'll cave sooner or later for the big money she's offering."

"Would Mona ever do that?"

"Never. And neither would I."

"Good. I hope you never sell it to her."

"You watch. Fabia will show up at Midsummer with some fancy-ass gift."

"She's invited, you mean?"

"No, never . . . but the bonfire is a public event. Everybody comes to that. Well . . . forty or fifty usually. Mostly folks from the village."

"That sounds charming," said Rhonda. "I can't wait."

29

THE WILFRED HE REMEMBERED

Michael thought it best not to make a coy joke when Wilfred offered him a tour of his bedroom. "Sure," he said brightly. "I'd love to see it. I hear it's Ali Baba's Cave."

"Is that what Mo told you?"

Michael grinned at him. "She meant it in the nicest way."

Wilfred opened a door and led the way into a high-ceilinged room draped with Persian carpets, obviously meant to suggest a pasha's tent. There were postcards and pictures pinned everywhere. Michael spotted himself among the photos—a shirtless summer shot taken up at the Yuba River when a conspiracy of shadows and late afternoon sun had made him look his best. He had hesitated before mailing it to Wilfred, so it was nice to see it here.

Over Wilfred's bed was a black-and-white poster of a man's face, half in shadow. The only color present was one piercing green eye. "That's striking," he said.

"That's George."

"Harrison? Is he trying out new facial hair or something?"

"George Michael, you philistine!"

"Oh . . . right . . . I can see that now. He's getting hotter all the time, isn't he?"

"I think he's just finally owning his sexuality, and that translates to hot when you wear it on the outside."

This remark struck Michael as more politically evolved than the Wilfred he remembered, the impish teenager for whom sex had just meant sex. He was a grown man now, and openness had become something to be valued.

"Is he out now?"

"Not yet, but I think he's about to be."

"What gives you that impression?"

"Well . . . I held his dick in me hand last month on Hampstead Heath."

Michael made a comic gaping face that hid what he immediately thought. *Of course this gorgeous cocoa-colored grown-up has graduated to doing it with global celebrities.*

Wilfred seemed to read his mind. "I don't really know him," he said. "It was at a cruising spot."

"Ah. Did you enjoy it?"

"Not really. He spooked me."

"Why?"

"He was wearing a mask. A wrestler's mask."

"Then how did you know it was him?"

"Someone told me later."

"That doesn't sound like he's very out to me."

"What's he gonna do, poor bloke? You can't have anonymous sex when you're not anonymous. I think it shows that he just wants to be with his mates."

Michael glanced up at the green-eyed icon above the bed. "That's a very sweet way to look at it," he said.

"He's coming out," said Wilfred. "Just as soon as he figures out that he can have it all."

"Wouldn't that be something." Michael looked back at Wilfred again. "Are they really still cruising on Hampstead Heath?"

"Why not? It's safer than going home with somebody. It's even safer than dogging."

"What's that?"

"You know . . . what the straight folks do. They park on a country lane with their wives and shag in the car while other people watch and wank."

Michael tilted his head dubiously. "You're serious? This is a thing?"

"It's very much a thing. There's a big car park behind the Esso in Cirencester that's packed with doggers when the pubs close. Big white bums pressed against the glass, feet sticking out of sunroofs, and . . . you name it."

"I'd rather not."

Wilfred smiled. "You have to pity them a bit. Life can get a little dull in the country for their kind."

"But not for you, I take it?" Michael knew this was a dangerous but necessary step.

"Well," said Wilfred, "I take the train into London every fortnight or so."

"That's good."

"And sometimes I bring talent home."

"Okay. And Mona is cool with that?"

"What do you think? One day I brought home a builder from

Bourton-on-the-Water and Mo served us breakfast in bed the next morning."

Michael felt pangs of jealousy in several directions, but shared only one. "She did that once when I brought someone home to Barbary Lane."

"No shit! When?"

"Oh . . . long time ago." That, of course, had been Jon, gone for a decade now, as hard as that was to take in. Mona had bestowed her breakfast-tray magic on them the morning after Michael brought Jon home to Barbary Lane. How dare she recycle that sacred family moment for some random builder in Bourton-on-the-Water? Some incredibly *hot* builder with a real tool belt and a hard body, who was younger than Michael by at least a decade.

Really, the nerve of that woman!

"She knows how to be charming," he said without further comment.

Michael had a revelation as they left the bedroom. He and Wilfred had talked about nothing but sex with other people since they'd come in this room. The meaning was clear: They were brothers now (or gay sisters, even), so passion between them was off-limits.

And they had never even kissed.

30

RIGHT NOW

Agolden dusk had settled over the great lawn as the gathering finally tucked into Rhonda's buttermilk fried chicken. The family was arrayed on quilted cotton blankets with cushions scattered here and there. Mona, who was sprawled next to Anna, grew concerned about her parent, who was propped up on one elbow and not looking at ease with it.

"Let me get you a chair. You can't be comfortable."

"No, no. I want to loll. I haven't lolled for years."

"There's a reason for that, dear heart."

"Be quiet. Don't rob me of my last chance to loll. I want to be Virginia Woolf lolling on the lawn." She stretched out languidly to make her point.

"Go ahead, Virginia," said Mona, pushing a cushion toward her, "but put that under your ass first."

Anna adjusted the cushion.

"And what do you mean by last chance?" asked Mona.

"Nothing dire, darling. I just mean . . . this . . . all this . . .

the wonder of this, right now." She gestured to the great golden house looming behind her. "It's what we've got right now, and it's so achingly beautiful, and it's all going to be gone in a flash, so let's just . . . be in the moment."

"I'm in the moment," said Mona. "Have you been in my stash?"

"No! You know I would have asked! Wilfred gave me an edible."

"I thought you were getting awfully metaphysical there."

Michael chuckled as all eyes turned to Wilfred. "A fella has to be hospitable," he said with a smirk.

"He was very gracious," said Anna.

Mona was mildly affronted. "Did you think I wouldn't bring weed to the picnic?"

Rhonda emerged from the house bearing a cooler of scrumpy.

"Bless you and sit down," said Mona. "We may never stand up again."

Rhonda did as she was told, but awkwardly, so Mona tossed a cushion to her. "We're lolling today," she said. "Thank you for this amazing fried chicken, Rhonda."

"Wilfred and I did it together," said Rhonda.

"You know that's not true," said Wilfred. "I was just her sous-chef."

Michael pulled a bottle of scrumpy from the cooler. "This looks good, Rhonda. What is it?"

"It's Mr. Hargis's famous scrumpy," said Rhonda. "He makes it from apples grown at Easley."

"What's scrumpy? And for that matter, who's Mr. Hargis?"

"You remember him," said Mona. "The old gardener. Sort of a family retainer who's not retaining much of anything, poor sod."

"Oh," said Anna. "I think I met him on my walk. He was in that little chapel feeling sad about the wife he lost."

"That would be Elspeth," said Wilfred. "She was a real battle-ax, but Mr. Hargis misses her just the same."

"How long has she been gone?" asked Rhonda.

"Oh . . . six or seven years, I guess."

"It must have been a great love," said Rhonda.

"Why do you say that?" asked Michael.

"Well . . . if she was that awful, but he still misses her . . . that sounds like love to me. People can still love deeply, even when they've stopped liking each other."

Mona rolled her eyes privately. Rhonda was obviously still trying to make a case for her abusive marriage to Ernie. The self-delusion was staggering—and deeply pitiable. Rhonda's bruises were still faintly visible, but she seemed to be clinging to the notion of reconciliation.

Mona resolved not to let that happen.

The scrumpy was a hit with everyone, a real head buzz that softened the edges of everything. Anna even dubbed it "the sin-semilla of ciders." Michael and Wilfred got chatty on the stuff, swapping boisterous tales about Earl's Court when they first met, about a dyke bar called Heds where they'd gone looking for Mona, about the gold ring in Lord Teddy's nipple that Michael found so comically alarming at the time. Rhonda received all this information with her face locked in a pleasant smile. She even laughed occasionally when she got the joke. She was trying her damnedest to be a part of all this, and that touched Mona deeply.

31

THEIR GO-BETWEEN

Rhonda was the first to leave the picnic. It wasn't that she hadn't enjoyed it. She just felt that these nice folks were a family with a shared history and needed some private time to themselves. Besides, two bottles of scrumpy had suddenly made her feel more spiritual. She wanted to be alone with her thoughts—and her Heavenly Father—in a quiet place.

Fortunately, Easley House was full of such places. She considered the library and even a window seat in the great hall, but settled on her own bedroom with a view of the folly and a door she could latch behind her. Unnecessary interruptions were the enemy of prayer. She moved the big wingback chair to a spot by the window and sank into it with a sigh. A breeze caressed her face, gentle as the hand of God. She closed her eyes and let the prayer seep out of her.

Gentle Jesus, I need your help. Ernie and I have been apart for a month now, and we've left so much unsettled. The people here have been so kind to me, and they think that Ernie is bad for me, and maybe they're

right, but they don't know Ernie the way I do. They don't even want
me to talk about him, because they think it just makes me hurt more.
They mean well, but they don't remember the Ernie I knew. They don't
know about the precious times we shared, the good things that happened
when we were young. I'm sure that some of that Ernie is still around,
but I never got the chance to find out because I shut him out of my life
so abruptly. So my question is this: Should I call him in Tarboro and at
least have a talk with him? If you think I should, please give me a sign.
Any sign will do. And thank you Jesus, for listening. Amen.

Rhonda remained in the chair long after her prayer was done.
She liked gazing out at the little dunce-capped folly turning
purple in the fading light. Down on the great lawn, there was
still intermittent laughter from the picnic, and Rhonda, to her
delight, could identify every laugh, including the soft chuckling
of Mona's stately mother, the woman they all called Anna.

The scrumpy had made her sleepy, so she moved to the bed
and, without undressing, pulled the covers over her. She fell
asleep almost instantly and dreamed of a long-ago summer when
she and Ernie had romped with their kids in the surf at Wrights-
ville Beach. She felt such contentment in the honeyed glow of
that dream that it jarred her to be rudely yanked from it by a
noise in the hallway—careful footsteps and the creaking of floor-
boards that always came with it in this ancient house. Wilfred (or
his visiting friend) was probably retreating to his bedroom after
too much scrumpy. Just like she had done.

"Good," she thought as she snuggled under the covers again.
"I won't be the only person up here."

She wasn't sure how long she slept, but when she woke there
was an envelope under her door. It was an official Easley House
envelope, the kind that Mona used when writing to guests. She

picked it up. It was addressed simply to Rhonda in a handwriting so familiar that it filled her with dread.

She went to the door, opened it, and looked in both directions. There was no one there. She stepped back into the room, closed and locked the door, then sat down in the wingback chair and opened the envelope. On a piece of Easley stationery she read this:

My beautiful bride,

Please don't be alarmed, but I am with you now.

The Lord told me to reach out to you. I just want a chance to explain things. If you can grant me this, come to our bench in the bluebell wood tonight at 9 p.m. Don't tell the others. They don't really know us.

I love you so much I can't live without you. You must know that.

ERNIE

Rhonda reread the note twice, trying to come to grips with it. How could this even be real? How long had Ernie been here, or had he never left at all? The idea was both comforting and terrifying. She hadn't done anything that couldn't be undone, and Ernie apparently hadn't given up on her yet. The words she came back to again and again was "our bench," as if that bench held sentimental significance for them as a couple. For her, it had been the place where love had gone to die, where she'd finally accepted the futility of loving Ernie.

And yet . . . maybe he realized that. Maybe that was precisely *why* he had chosen that bench for a reunion. Maybe he wanted to make things right again on the very spot where their marriage had finally gone off the rails. She had sat in this very chair less than an hour ago and asked Jesus for one more chance to talk to Ernie again. And—Hallelujah—Ernie had done the exact same thing. Their go-between had been Jesus. And Jesus, in his infinite wisdom, told them both to let love rule their hearts.

If that wasn't a miracle, what was?

There was only one way to find out.

32

WHAT IF

The party had finally migrated from the darkening lawn into the great hall, so Wilfred began disrobing the upright piano, yanking away a swath of worn blue velvet that Mona had put there last year as a dustcover.

"Who plays?" asked Michael.

"I was hoping one of you might."

"Nope. Sorry. And Mona, forget it. She hates these uprights."

"I know," said Wilfred, smiling. "They remind her of her Gran's knocking shop in Nevada."

Michael laughed. "You know about that, huh?"

"Oh, yeah."

"Everything reminds her of something. It's exhausting."

Wilfred sat down at the piano. "Shall I play something for you."

"Play? Since when?"

"Since you've been gone, mate. Mo bought this thing so we could take lessons from an old biddy who came here twice a week. Mona tangled with her about Thatcher, so she never made it past the first week. I stayed long enough to learn this . . ." Wilfred plinked out a few opening chords.

"I know this one. It's Satie, isn't it? So bittersweet and simple."

"Well, it's simple to play anyway. Do you know why it's called Gymnopédie?

"Nope."

"A gymnopédie was an annual festival in ancient Greece where the young men danced with each other naked."

"You're shitting me? The piano teacher told you this."

"Fuck, no. I learned it from a trick in London."

"So . . . Satie was queer?"

"Well, it was 1886, so he was . . . what's the word? . . . discrete, but he dropped hairpins everywhere in his music. This was one of them."

"No wonder I've always liked it."

Wilfred stopped playing.

"Don't stop. I'm picturing the naked youths."

"That's all I know, mate."

"Well, phooey."

Mona yelled from across the great hall, where she was sitting with Anna. "Come join us, boys. I've made tea so we can sober up."

"Do we have to?" Michael yelled back.

"If you want weed, you have to detox from the scrumpy."

"She's such a bossy-boots," Michael said to Wilfred.

"I heard that," yelled Mona.

———

They were all at the big table now, drinking tea.

"Where's Rhonda?" asked Wilfred.

"I think she's retired to her chambers," said Mona.

"That's a shame," said Anna. "She's such a nice woman."

"Yes she is. But let's not summon her. The weed might be too much for her."

"Why?"

"She's a devout church lady."

"Ah. Well then, that's very thoughtful of you. Marijuana should never overrule good manners."

Michael grinned. "That should be stitched onto a sampler."

Anna smiled back at him. "It's just the truth."

Mona removed a shiny blue cigarette case from the pocket of her jeans jacket. "Now," she said, "there's one for each of us, out of deference to the Mother of Us All."

"You remembered," said Anna, raising her hand to her chest.

"Of course," said Mona, opening the case and offering it to her parent.

Anna took a joint and lit it. "Did you grow this here?"

"Technically, yes."

"Technically?"

"Lord Teddy sent me some seeds from San Francisco."

"How thoughtful," said Anna. "Then the first toke should be in his honor."

They all lit their joints with the lighter on the table. "To Lord Teddy," said Wilfred, "who left for California in search of his dream."

There was a volley of "Lord Teddys" all around as tokes were taken. Wilfred noticed that afterward a shadow passed over Michael's face.

"Whatcha thinking?" he asked.

"I dunno. Just that I'm sorry I lost touch with him in San Francisco. He was driving a cab for a while and seemed to love the freedom of that. But after that . . . we just lost touch. I didn't even know he was sick, until I read his obit in the *BAR*."

Anna reached across the table and took Michael's hand. "You mustn't punish yourself, dear. It accelerates so ruthlessly. No one can keep up with it."

"And you've had your own worries," Mona added.

"He still deserved better," said Michael glumly.

"Stop that, you little dipshit. You can blame yourself for anything. Teddy had his own friends there, and he was hell-bent on living in San Francisco long before he met you. How could you be expected to save him from something you haven't even escaped yourself?"

An embarrassed silence fell. Wilfred did his best to lighten things up. "Excuse me," he said, grinning at Michael. "Did my mother just call you a dipshit?"

"It's a term of endearment," said Mona.

"Yeah," said Michael grinning. "Like asswipe. Which is what she called me this morning."

Anna arched an eyebrow at Mona. "That does sound a tad angry, dear."

"Maybe . . . but it's not directed at him."

Anna took that in, then shifted to pleasantries, like pot growing in England and how thrilling it must be to live in the land of Dickens and Tennyson and Isherwood.

"But Isherwood moved to California," said Michael.

Anna shrugged and took another delicate toke. "We're all portable, dear. Take a look at the people at this table. We're from everywhere, but we're here right now. That's what happens when you're living your truth."

"Ah," Mona said under her breath, "the wise one speaks."

When the women had finally gone up to their rooms, Wilfred turned to Michael and said: "Any idea why Mo had her knickers in a twist tonight?"

Michael grinned. "Oh, same old, same old. Scattershot anger. AIDS has taken most of the men she's ever known, including, I suppose . . . me . . . eventually. She's pissed about that, so, naturally, she takes it out on me. That's Mona. We men are always letting her down."

"I know that one. She got cross with me just for going into Soho."

Michael laughed.

"But it seems to me," Wilfred added, "there's something else eating her. Why was she cross with Anna?"

Michael hesitated. "I don't know if I should tell you this."

"C'mon, mate, it's Wilfred, your pen pal."

"Okay . . . I overheard them in the library this morning. Mona asked Anna to come live here, and Anna, very gently, turned her down. I missed some of it, because I hightailed it out of there before they could see me."

"I figured it was something like that."

Michael smiled at him. "You know Anna would never leave Barbary Lane."

"Well, I do and you do, and probably Mo does, too. I guess she thought it was worth a shot. She loves Easley, but she needs her old family sometimes. I do me best, of course, but I'm only one person."

"She couldn't have a better person," said Michael, gripping Wilfred's arm affectionately.

"Let me show you something," said Wilfred.

"Okay."

Wilfred led the way up the stairs and down a hallway that Michael had never seen. Halfway down, Wilfred opened a small door that required Michael to stoop as he entered.

"What the hell is this?" he asked.

"It's me secret lair," said Wilfred. "Have a seat."

It was a small room, no bigger than a large closet, completely padded with old mattresses. At one end was a low railing overlooking the great hall down below.

"This is the minstrels' gallery," Michael said after a moment. "This is where I saw Mona when we took that tour."

"You're quick," said Wilfred. "I added the mattresses, of course."

"Do I have to ask what goes on in here?"

"You're the first bloke I've ever brought here. Go on, stretch out. Make yourself comfortable."

Michael did as he was told, sinking into a body-shaped indentation in the mattresses. Wilfred lay beside him, not touching but close enough that Michael caught a whiff of his bay rum. They were both silent for a moment. Then Wilfred said: "I wanna be naked with you."

"Wilfred . . ."

"Shut your cakehole. I know what you're gonna say. You're going home next week, and we're more like brothers than lovers, and it might spoil our friendship, and all that shit. But what if you go home and die . . . and what if I do, for that matter . . . and what if we've missed out on our one chance to be that much closer to each other."

Michael was stunned into silence.

"And if you don't fancy me, it won't hurt me feelings, but I had to give it a try at least."

Michael rolled over and looked Wilfred in the eye.

"Of course I fancy you, silly. I've fancied you since it was against the law."

"But?"

"No buts. No buts at all."

He leaned in and kissed Wilfred softly on the lips. Then he reached for Wilfred's cock and pulled him closer.

33

THE GOOD KIND OF CRAZY

Rhonda slipped out of her room just before eleven and tippy-toed down the hall. Anna and Mona had already retired to their rooms, and the menfolk were nowhere to be seen, so there was little reason to fret. Besides, she lived here now, sort of, and she could always say that she was heading down to the kitchen for a late-night snack.

Her heart was pounding wildly, so much so that she halfway hoped Mona would wake up and catch her and put an end to this recklessness. Mona was her best friend now, as unlikely as that seemed, and she would know what to do.

An almost-full moon was seeping through the stained-glass window in the great hall, and there were still embers glowing in the fireplace. As she crossed the room, she caught sight of several mice skittering across the table in search of crumbs. "Just the cleanup crew" is what Mona would say, no doubt, and the Lord would just have to forgive her for that.

The easiest part was leaving the house, since she used the door that had never, to her recollection, been locked. Once outside, she adjusted the cream satin cocktail dress that Ernie had bought her at Harrods, and set off across the great lawn, flashlight in hand. She knew that the bluebell wood began on a bark path beside the barn, so she headed in that direction. She had never been to the wood at night, so the darkness surprised her. These trees were slender, and not very tall, but their leafiness all but obliterated the moonlight.

The bark path led her deeper into the wood until she spotted the bench, less than twenty feet away. Her heart leapt when she saw that someone was sitting there, facing away from her. She didn't point her flashlight at him for fear of startling him, but waited until she was close enough to call his name quietly.

"Ernie?"

The figure spun around. "Thank God," he said. "I prayed you would come."

His face was unshaven and haggard. He was wearing his nice gray travel suit, but it was soiled and ripped in several places.

"I'm sorry," he said, upon seeing her expression. "I wanted to clean up for you, but . . ."

Her heart was aching for him. "Where have you been, Ernie?"

"Here. Well, around here. Mr. Hargis lets me sleep in the chapel. He understands what it's like for a man to lose his lady love."

"Have you been here the whole time?"

He nodded. "I never went back to London."

"Goodness, Ernie." It was all she could think to say.

"I know . . . but I thought I would lose you for good if I didn't stay. Does that sound crazy to you?"

She didn't answer. It did sound crazy, but the good kind of crazy. It sounded like someone who was deeply in love.

"Would you sit down?" said Ernie. "I know I stink to high heaven, but . . ."

She sank to the bench, but kept her distance. Her cocktail dress was the very opposite of Ernie's ravaged jacket. That made sense. She was always overdressing for events with him.

"You know," he said quietly, gazing down, "that was really a dirty trick you played on me. That all of you played on me. I'm a decent, God-fearing man who did not deserve the humiliation of that. I was halfway to London, when it dawned on me what you'd done. Then I got the first train back to Moreton-in-Marsh and licked my wounds at the Black Bear. The bartender remembered me . . . remembered us."

He gazed up at her with bleary eyes. "It's amazing how men can help one another out when there's trouble with a woman."

Trouble with a woman. Was that how he saw the end of their marriage?

"Why did you reach out to me, Ernie? To tell me how much I've hurt you?"

"No!"

"Then what?"

"To . . . tell you . . . that I love you, and I want you back . . . and I want to leave this nest of sinners and for you to come home to Tarboro with me."

"Actually," she said, "I'm enjoying myself in this nest of sinners. And they need me here, which is more than I can say for you . . . or Tarboro."

"What could you possibly do for them?"

"I cook. I clean. I garden. I've worked wonders for this place."

"Has she turned you? Is that's what's happened?"

"Turned me?"

"You know she's a lesbian, don't you?"

"Of course I know that. Everybody knows that."

He blinked at her, slack mouthed.

"Mona is the kindest person I've ever met," she said.

"So that's your reason for leaving me?"

"That's one of them. I never knew what it felt like to be treated with kindness until I lived here with her and Wilfred. And don't tell me that he's a gay, too, because I know that already and I don't give a hoot. It's my job as a Christian not to give a hoot."

Ernie glared at her in disbelief. "They've completely corrupted you, woman. You're in league with the devil now."

"And I'll tell you something else," Rhonda went on. "If I was ever to sleep with a woman, it would be someone like Mona. Someone who didn't slap me around for twenty years and make me have to wear makeup to hide my bruises. Someone who doesn't berate me in front of our friends! Someone who's loving and could give me an actual orgasm, for once."

She knew that last part would be too much for him, and it was. After gaping at her in disbelief, he yanked her to her feet and slugged her in the face with a full fist, not just his flat palm. It was the first time he had ever done that, and for one gruesome moment, she thought it might be the last. She had heard something crack as her head fell to one side, so she stayed perfectly still in that position, while he shook her limp body. *If he thinks I'm dead, he'll stop.*

"Goddamn it, Rhonda, wake up. I didn't hit you that hard."

She opened her eyes and spat at him.

"You common Cherokee bitch!"

He was hauling off to hit her again when a figure sprang from the shadows and threw him to the ground. "Leave her alone, you bastard!"

Rhonda sank to the bench again and watched as Ernie's head was pounded repeatedly against the ground. She didn't have the energy to tell this man to stop.

When Ernie was completely still, her rescuer rose to his feet.

"Are you okay?"

She nodded. "Is he?"

"I don't think so," he said. "Go back to the house."

He was old and craggy and had a gold ring in his ear.

For some reason, she knew to obey him.

34

THE PLOT THICKENS

Michael and Wilfred were still together in the minstrels' gallery, letting the moment last as long as it could, when a noise startled them.

"What's that?" whispered Michael.

"Just the door. Someone's coming in."

Far below them, a sobbing figure crossed the floor of the great hall and headed up the stairs. It was Rhonda.

"What was she doing outdoors?" asked Wilfred.

"Beats the fuck out of me."

"Should we see what's up?"

"I think she's heading up to see Mona for some girl time."

Michael shot him a look.

"I mean," said Wilfred, "you know, shoulder crying."

"Oh . . . well . . . okay. I thought there was something I didn't know about."

Wilfred shrugged. "I think they'd make a fine couple, actually. One cooks and cleans while the other one raises hell and wars with the world."

Michael wrinkled his brow slyly. "What's that? A little Aboriginal wisdom?"

Wilfred chuckled and gently gathered Michael's cock and balls in his hand. "Are you demeaning my people?"

"We're queers, we don't have a people, Wilfred. We're our own people. And we get to choose every damn thing we do. Right?"

Wilfred buried his face in Michael's neck. "We don't have to stay here, you know. We could go to a bed somewhere."

"Yes, but that would entail unsticking from you, which I really don't want to do, not to mention finding my clothes, which won't be easy. I'm pretty sure my jockstrap and one of my socks just landed on the ballroom floor."

Wilfred chuckled. "Then we'll stay here." He plumped up the mattresses to make a nest for both of them. "C'mon. Settle in. Consider me chest your pillow."

They lay there in silence for the longest time, listening to the creaks and groans of the old house. Finally Wilfred said: "Do you worry about how much time you have left?"

"You mean here or . . . in general."

"In general."

"Well, sure . . . of course. But I try not to dwell on it. Otherwise I'd be wasting the time that I do have."

"Makes sense."

"No, it doesn't. None of it makes sense. It's all such a rat fuck."

Wilfred squeezed him tighter and petted his back. "Are you planning on leaving Thack?"

"That's over," said Michael.

"You know I can't leave Easley."

"I know you can't leave Mona, and I'm glad about that. She needs you. You're the best relationship she's ever had."

"I suppose that's true."

"I know it is. I've known her for a long time."

Wilfred drew a line with his finger across Michael's back. "Of course, you and Anna could always come live here."

"If that's an offer, it's the best I've had all year, but . . . Anna would never leave Barbary Lane, and—"

"—you could never leave Anna."

"Pretty much."

"I guess that's it, then. Midsummer will have to be good."

There were urgent footsteps on the stairs, as Rhonda returned with Mona in tow.

"The plot thickens," whispered Michael.

The women headed out the door into the garden. Mona mumbled something to Rhonda before they left, but Michael couldn't make it out.

"Any idea about what just happened?" asked Wilfred.

"I'd say it was some sort of pagan ritual, but I don't think Rhonda would put up with that."

They both got a laugh out of that.

35

MR. SCAMP

Flashlight in hand, Rhonda led the way into the bluebell wood. Mona was hot on her heels, already imagining the worst.

"Are you sure he's dead?" she asked.

"Yeah."

"What about the man who killed him?"

"What about him?"

"Will he still be there?"

"I have no idea."

"And you've never seen him before?"

"No."

Mona turned the flashlight toward the bench, preparing for a gruesome scene. There wasn't a body in sight.

"Are you sure it was here?"

"Well . . . maybe over to the left there."

"Rhonda, there's no one here."

"This makes no sense at all."

"Maybe he just left of his own accord. Maybe he wasn't dead after all."

"You think I'm delirious?"

"No! Of course not. I just . . . let's just sit down for moment and collect ourselves."

Mona sank to the bench and motioned Rhonda to do the same.

"I just don't get it," Rhonda said.

"Well, we're not going to figure it out here. Let's go back to the house and have a nice cup of tea."

Mona had never uttered that phrase to anyone, but without another word, the two of them rose and followed the bark path back to the house. It was really the only thing to do. Rhonda might not be delirious, but she was definitely in shock. At the very least, she needed to feel safe inside.

As they passed the barn, a man stepped out of the shadows. "Beg pardon, Lady Roughton!"

His face looked like it was made of granite. He had a big gold earring in one ear.

"This is him!" cried Rhonda. "The man who rescued me."

The man extended his hand. "I'm Thomas Scamp."

"Scamp," said Mona, taking his hand. "Isn't that a Romani name?"

"Yes, milady."

"Don't call me that, please, I'm Mona . . . I once bought a beautiful bracelet from a woman outside of Stow. Her name was Scamp."

"That would be me daughter, Ethelinda."

"Yes, course. Ethelinda Scamp. Such a distinctive name . . .

and she was very nice to me. So how did you come to save my friend's life?"

Mona thought it best to be as diplomatic and unhysterical about this as possible.

Mr. Scamp said: "I walk in your woods sometimes. It's near to our wagons, and it's always so peaceful. I hope it's not . . ."

"That's fine. No problem. I understand."

So I was there earlier tonight, when I heard this woman having the bejesus beat out of her, so I ran over and tore the man off her. I guess I banged his head on the ground a few times."

"You killed him?"

"I don't know if I was the actual cause, but he was dead when I was done with him."

Mona suppressed a smile. Talk about a line that would never hold up in court.

"So, Mr. Scamp . . . what have you done with his body?"

"The dead gent, you mean?"

"Yes."

"I'm holdin' him for safekeepin'."

"Okaay," she said. *Whatever that means.*

"You know, away from the animals. Rats and such. He would make a fine dinner for the critters. I mean no disrespect."

"None taken," said Rhonda, entering the discussion and shaking his gnarled hand. "I'm Mrs. Blaylock."

Mr. Scamp did a noticeable double take, landing on Rhonda in the end. "You mean? He was your husband?"

Rhonda nodded ruefully. "Didn't look like it, did it?"

Mr. Scamp shook his head. "It looked like he was trying to kill you,"

"He was," said Rhonda. "I have to thank you, Mr. Scamp."

"That's okay," he replied.

It occurred to Mona suddenly that this stately gentleman before her must be the very same "Old Gypsy" Mr. Hargis claimed to have chased out of every building on the estate. Mona knew that was an exaggeration, a conceit designed to make the old gardener look like he was doing his job, but it didn't matter at the moment. What mattered now was that Mr. Hargis, with his failing mind and sentimental Scottish streak, had harbored Ernie in the chapel for the past six weeks. So Mr. Hargis must never learn about Ernie's fate.

"We will not be reporting this to the police, Mr. Scamp."

Mr. Scamp nodded and mumbled in agreement. Any sort of tangle with the police never turned out to be good news for the Romani folk around here.

"This should be strictly a family affair." Mona continued. "By which I mean my family and your family. It never goes any further. Are we in agreement?"

"We are," said Mr. Scamp. "Completely."

"Would you like to join us in the house for a glass of brandy?"

"Thank you kindly," he said, "but I must be on my way. There's business to attend to."

She assumed he meant the body.

In the kitchen Mona grabbed a bottle of brandy and two glasses and headed up to her bedroom with Rhonda. It was the safest place to decompress without Wilfred and Michael hearing them. She poured two glasses and downed one on the spot.

"What a night, eh?"

"I'm still shaking," said Rhonda, holding out her hand as proof.

"Drink that," said Mona, indicating the other glass of brandy.

Rhonda obeyed, making a medicine face when she had finished.

"Now . . . we need to take stock of things. We're the only ones who know that Ernie was here, right? Not Wilfred or Michael? And, presumably, no one back in North Carolina?"

"Right. I told my sister he was probably headed to France to visit a military cemetery."

"Great. We're covered then."

"But why can't we just say that Mr. Scamp was defending me, and killed him accidentally."

"That's a whole different can of worms. The Romani don't like dealing with the police. And for good reason."

"I'm sorry. . . . The who?"

"Mr. Scamp and his large family are Romani travelers. They used to be called Gypsies, because ignorant Victorians thought they came from Egypt, but we're more civilized than that now. Mr. Hargis is just too old to know better.

Rhonda's mouth went slack, as if in shock that her unreconstructed Confederate husband had been offed by a real live Gypsy. Mona, for her part, found justice in that.

"And here's the beauty part: you don't have to go back to Tarboro and explain all this to Ernie's friends and family. It's a clean break from a bad marriage, and you get to be free at last. The rest of your life can begin."

"But . . . won't they come here looking for him?"

"So what? There isn't a crime without a body, and I'm very good at keeping a straight face. We can say we watched him get on the train, so . . . he must have disappeared somewhere in Europe after he left here."

Rhonda poured herself another glass of brandy and swigged it. "This is crazy," she said, setting the glass down.

"You're right," said Mona. "But I think it'll work."

Mona deposited Rhonda at her bedroom door and headed up the stairs to the attic. If ever there was an issue to be taken to the Jury, this was it.

They were hanging on their usual rafter, furry brown wings tipped with moonlight. At Mona's approach they rustled in unison, but more in greeting than alarm.

She did a quick head count. "Well, looks like you're all here. Plus maybe a few cousins from the hills. You know what I'm here about, don't you?"

Rustle, rustle.

"Right. Can't get anything past you. So . . . do you think I should do it?"

Silence.

"I hear you. There are lots of ways it could fuck up, but I just can't . . . you know, think what they are right now."

Rustle, rustle.

"You can't either, huh. Then you think I should go ahead?"

Rustle, rustle, rustle.

"Okay, okay. I'm on it."

She returned to her bedroom, to find a fully hammered Rhonda waiting outside the door. "Do you mind if I sleep with you tonight? I just can't be alone right now."

Mona studied her face for a moment. "What side do you sleep on?"

"The left side, I guess."

"That's mine, too. But you can have it tonight."

They went to the bed and climbed in fully clothed, pulling the quilt over them. They both were bone weary from this nightmare of a day.

"Things will look better in the morning," said Mona, though she knew very well that might not be true at all.

The last injury Ernie Blaylock would ever inflict on his wife had just begun to bloom on her face.

36

WE HUMANS

At dawn on Midsummer Day, Mr. Scamp emerged from the woods and met Mona at the kitchen door, as planned, with four of his solemn, sloe-eyed grandsons in tow. She recognized the oldest one, a pretty teenager who'd been playing "Yesterday" on a battered guitar the day she bought the bracelet from Ethelinda Scamp. The juxtaposition of that modern tune and that antique painted wagon made her feel the full, majestic sweep of a family that had been on the move for a thousand years, even since they left Northern India. That was a record that Lord Teddy's ancient housebound family had not come close to touching.

Mr. Scamp came straight to the point. "Job's done," he said.

"Thank you so much, Mr. Scamp."

"Thank *you*," he said.

The subtext of this exchange was so strong that she felt compelled to add: "I'm so glad we were able to help each other out."

He just nodded solemnly.

"Were you able to find the fennel?"

"Oh, yes. And plenty of it, too. Grows wild all over the place. I left it in the clearing."

"That's terrific. Thanks. You're a good man."

"I do me best."

"So . . . go get some sleep. I'm sure you all need it."

"Thank you, milady."

She didn't bother to correct him this time. Right now he could call her whatever she damn well wanted.

S he needed sleep herself, so she fell into bed as the ground fog was clearing from the lawn. She awoke after nine to find Rhonda in the great hall making ivy laurels for the celebrants.

"Those look pretty," she said. "Aren't you clever?"

"I'm just winging it," said Rhonda. "What time are we expecting people?"

"You never know. They come straggling in during the day, most just to get a peek at the house. The bonfire isn't lit until midafternoon, and some won't even stay for that. Just give them a laurel and tell 'em to feel free to wander the grounds. Do not let them in the house under any circumstances. A few years back a Georgian candlestick went missing."

Mona was reminded of an artful plywood sign—a whimsical fairy pointing to the woods—that Poppy had created last year to steer the public away from the house. She felt a little twinge of guilt when she dug it out of the hall closet, but she saw no reason not to use it again. Relationships came and went. Art was just art, in the end.

———

B y noon, she had moved the laurels to a bridge table on the great lawn. Moments later Wilfred approached with a smirk on his face.

"Well, guess who just invaded the house with an obscenely large basket of exotic fruits?"

"Fabia Dane. Did you get her out quickly?"

"I tried, but she was busy charming Michael with her twatty rich-bitch ways."

"Michael can't stand her. Has he completely forgotten the last time he was here?"

"I think he was just being nice."

"That's always been his problem. He suffers fools gladly. Leave me alone now. I've got laurels to give out."

"You need help?"

"Nope. Not a bit. The Scamp boys have volunteered their services for the day."

"Who the hell are the Scamp boys?"

"Tell you later, if you're good."

Wilfred straggled off, looking confused. Mona felt sure that he and Michael had consummated their pen-pal romance two nights earlier, but so far there had been no announcements, and Mona knew better than to ask. Boys could be so funny some-times.

As soon as Wilfred disappeared into the woods Fabia came swooping in.

"Mona, darling."

Then, without a trace of irony, she did an actual double air kiss, making Mona withdraw instinctively. The woman was truly without shame.

"Did you get the fruit basket?"

"Oh yes. Wilfred said you brought it yourself."

"Oh . . . well . . . yes, you can't really trust the local post with luxury items."

Fruit is a luxury item?

"It looks quite grand," said Mona. "You really shouldn't have."

"I know," said Fabia, "but it's Midsummer, and we must all do our best to honor the grand old lady that is Easley."

Barf.

O h," Fabia added blithely, "did you know you're pinned to the wall in the post office?"

Mona had been fully expecting this news. She just hadn't expected to hear it from the hateful Fabia Dane.

"Oh . . . that photograph, you mean?"

"Did you consent to that?"

No, she held me at gunpoint and forced me to lie down in a creek.

"Why? Didn't you like it?" asked Mona.

"I don't think my opinion is important."

"But?"

"I just don't think a civil servant—a postmistress, for heaven's sake—should have artistic pretensions that she inflicts on the public at her place of work. She's a tragic little thing, isn't she? One has to feel just a bit sorry for her."

"Does one?"

"Well, what did you think of that photograph?"

"I rather liked it, if you must know. She was looking for a redhead to play Lizzie Siddal, so I volunteered. She had nothing at all to work with, including me, and she made something wonderful out of it."

"Well, if you're not embarrassed, far be it from me to—"

"Do you even know who Lizzie Siddal *was*?"

"Can't say that I do."

"Then I suggest you stop being an art critic, and make yourself useful." She picked up a wreath of pansies and ivy, handing it in Fabia's direction. "Here, have a laurel. Make a wish and dance around the fire three times with a stone in your pocket. It'll make everything better."

Fabia stiffened visibly. "Thank you. I may do that."

"And don't bother sharing the wish with me. I already know what it is."

Fabia gave her a curdled smile and walked away.

Mona knew it was foolhardy to taunt Fabia about her never-ending lust for Easley, but it felt pretty fucking wonderful to do it.

This house was Mona's and always would be.

Shortly after two, she headed into the woods to check on the work the Scamp boys had done overnight. The bonfire clearing was neater than she had ever seen it, raked free of old ashes, with half a dozen folding chairs from the barn placed around the edges for the use of the elderly and infirm. There was a pile of wish stones near the entrance to the clearing, and the wild fennel she had requested was stacked as neatly as possible near the edge of the fire pit. The fire structure itself was nearly as tall as she was, rectangular in shape and built of sturdy cross-hatched timber that could be easily lit through a tinder-filled hole in the bottom.

She sat down on one of the chairs and gave herself a moment of peace and reflection.

This was the right thing to do for Rhonda, who needed the violence and strife to stop and not follow her home to North Carolina.

It was the right thing to do for Mr. Scamp, who should not be punished for his lifesaving good deed.

And how perfect it was to do it on Midsummer Day, when the fires of the season are meant to burn away the past and make room for new growth.

And wasn't it right to keep Wilfred, Michael, and Anna out of the loop? Why give them the burden of carrying such a secret when she and Rhonda could carry it alone.

Mona was pondering all these things when Miss Vanilla Wafer came loping into the clearing.

"Hey, Nilla," she crooned, opening her arms in greeting, "How's my little suffragette?"

But Nilla barely knew Mona was there. The dog was following a scent, her nose held high, as she sniffed her way around the fire structure, finally landing on a spot.

"Oh shit," said Mona. "Don't do that."

But Nilla abruptly sat down and lifted a paw to scratch at the fire structure. Then she uttered a noise that was almost, but not quite, a whimper. Mona's heart was breaking. She sat down next to Nilla and put her arm across her.

"Yes, that's him," she murmured. "You found him. That's a good girl, that's a very clever girl. So let's just pay our respects and be gone before the ceremony begins."

The dog was unmoving.

"I know you liked him. And he liked you, too. He just was really shitty when it came to human beings. You know?"

Nilla made that noise again.

"You're right," said Mona. "Humans are fucked up."

Nilla turned and looked at Mona with the same defeated look she used for baths in the kitchen sink. Then she sighed to drive the point home.

"You know what? I'm pretty sure there are treats at the house."

The t-word did the trick, as it always did. Nilla rose to her feet, shook herself out, and followed her mistress out of the clearing.

She would stay in the house until the bonfire was over.

37

A MONA THING

Michael and Wilfred arrived at the bonfire shortly after three o'clock. By that time the fire was burning so high and fierce that the circling celebrants had to stand well back to escape the wall of heat and leaping flames. Michael had expected something much more tame, something more like a campfire, certainly not this raging inferno.

"Holy shit," he said.

Wilfred shrugged. "It *is* a cleansing ritual."

"And who are these people?" There were at least a dozen of them moving around the fire in a counterclockwise dance.

"Just locals. That blond boy over there is the vicar's son, the one I wrote you about."

"Oh yeah. The one who came home with you just to see the house."

"Can you blame him?"

"Well, no . . . but . . . fuck him and his ulterior motives. I would have come home with you if you lived in a hovel. Especially knowing what I know now."

Wilfred smirked. "Don't embarrass me. Truth is, most of these people are here for the house. It's an annual thing we do for goodwill in the village."

Two men entered the clearing with an enormous log that they flung into the fire. It sent sparks flying into the sky and brought a primal cheer from the celebrants.

"Who are those guys?"

"Just some local blokes that Mo found."

"Do they specialize in bonfires or something?"

"I've no idea, but they've been at it all day."

"It looks like someone has."

"Shall we collect our wish stones?"

"Sure thing."

They went to a pile of stones near the edge of the clearing. Each of them took a stone and put it in his pocket.

"What now?" asked Michael.

"Make a wish, but don't share it."

"Okay." Michael closed his eyes for a moment. Wasn't there a rule that wishes should never be made with your eyes open?

"Now," said Wilfred, "you just walk around the bonfire three times, then toss your wish stone into the fire."

They joined the procession around the fire. There were giggling young women and stodgy older ones in harlequin glasses. At the moment Michael and Wilfred were the only men.

"Is this really a pagan thing?" Michael asked.

"I think it's largely a Mona thing."

Michael smiled. "She made it up."

"Who knows? Does it really matter?"

After three circumnavigations they flung their wish stones into the fire and retreated to the folding chairs at the edge of the clearing. The fire wasn't as fierce as it was before, but it was still burning bright as twilight approached.

"So what did you wish for?" asked Michael.

"I don't think you're supposed to ask that. But never mind . . . I wished that you would keep on living."

Michael turned and looked at him. "Just that? Just that I wouldn't die?"

"Pretty much. What was yours?"

"Is it awful that I wished the same thing?"

"That you wouldn't die?"

"Yes. It's just that life is so sweet right now." He reached out and took Wilfred's hand. "To be here in this unbelievable place. To have the love of a couple of old friends that I cherish . . ." He squeezed Wilfred's hand. "And have really hot sex with another old friend. I just want to keep feeling these things, that's all. I can't help it. I want more of this life."

Wilfred smiled at him. "Thanks for that review."

"You're welcome. I mean it."

They remained there, holding hands. One of the fire tenders came into the clearing and threw something into the fire.

"What do you think that is?" said Michael.

"Fennel."

"Like in a salad? What's it for?"

"Aromatherapy, according to Mona. It's supposed to neutralize the smoke . . . or something like that."

"That makes no sense at all."

"Well . . . consider the source."

They both laughed.

38

RUNNING EASLEY

While dozens of strangers were invading the garden, Mona and Rhonda were holed up in the library drinking tea.

"Shouldn't we head out to the bonfire?" asked Rhonda.

"Not really," said Mona.

"Why not?"

"It's just a lot of hokum for the locals. I usually end up having to talk to someone deeply boring. Trust me, we aren't missing a thing."

"Okay, then."

"And c'mon, do you really want to be dealing with the public right now?"

"I guess not. No. You're right."

"You must be completely wrung out."

"I guess I am. Sort of."

Mona lifted the teapot and filled Rhonda's cup. "I've been meaning to talk to you about something," she said.

"Yes?"

"Are you really prepared to go back to America?"

Rhonda thought about that. "No . . . but I must."

"Why must you? Your children are grown and living elsewhere. I know you have a sister there, but she has a life of her
own. You'll just spend your days with people who want to be-
moan the mysterious disappearance of your husband. Even if
they don't talk about it to your face, it will be there, coloring
your life until the day you die. And you'll have to put on a brave
face about a man who tried to kill you. You'll have to pretend
that you're in mourning for a monster. Ernie will rule your life
even after death."

"Well . . . maybe so, but—"

"Hear me out. What if you called your sister and told her
that Ernie called from France to say that he's not coming back
to England, and you have no problem with that, since you were
already planning to leave him? That's right, isn't it?"

"Yes. I told her that the last time we talked."

"Great. So now you tell her you're staying in England, because you've found a wonderful job and you love this country
and you want to stay."

"And the wonderful job?"

Mona threw up her hands as if the answer were obvious.
"Running Easley!"

"What?"

"Oh, I'll still be the lady of the manor, because that's what the
tourists want. But you can be the House Manager or the Domestic Czar or whatever the fuck you want to call yourself. And you
won't be doing it for free either. We'll work out an equitable split
of the profits. Your talents are worth something to me, Rhonda.
This house looks better than it's looked in years, and I know you

can work more wonders if I just turn you loose on it. We'll have to get you a visa so you can stay, but I don't think that'll be a problem if Lady Roughton vouches for you. And need I mention that Wilfred fucking loves this idea."

"I don't know what to say," said Rhonda.

"A simple yes will do."

"Then yes! I do! I mean . . . not I do . . . but whatever . . . I *will*."

They were both laughing when Nilla came loping into the room to elicit a chin scratch from Rhonda.

"See there?" said Mona. "It's unanimous."

Rhonda embraced the dog like an old friend.

"And now," said Mona, "I think it's time for Miss Vera."

"Who?"

Mona tapped the side of her face to signal Rhonda's bruise.

"Oh," said Rhonda. "Is it hideous?"

"Nah," said Mona. "Nothing Miss Vera can't handle."

39

CLOSE ENOUGH FOR NOW

On the morning the visitors left Easley for the train station, Mona had a proposition for her departing parent: "Would you walk up to the folly with me, Anna?"

Anna cast a dubious glance at the little gazebo on top of the hill. "Up there, you mean?"

"I know it's a climb, but I'm asking for a reason."

"I'm a little worried about the cab."

"It's just ol' Colin. He'll wait if he has to. And he's not coming for half an hour."

"All right then! Onward!"

They strode up the stone steps together, with Anna leading the way and setting the pace. The old woman was barely out of breath when they reached the top.

"You're such an athlete," said Mona, sinking into a canvas chair.

Anna pulled up a chair next to her and sat down. "I suppose the Barbary Steps have helped with that. Oh, look at the view!"

The house was something of a toy from this height, and most of the land around it was visible from the folly. To Mona's delight, Anna could already identify the gatehouse, the chapel, the old barn, and the bluebell wood. The great circle where the bonfire had been was now satisfyingly flat and gray, having been raked clean by an army of Scamps. Another big summer rain and grass would be sprouting there again, fine as the fuzz on a newborn's head.

"I see why you brought me here," said Anna.

"It's lovely, isn't it? But it wasn't about the view."

"Then . . . what?"

"Well . . . you've been everywhere else at Easley and . . . I'll always have the memories of that . . . I just didn't want a single place here that I can't associate with you."

"You funny child," said Anna. "You brought me up here so I could mark it?"

"Pretty much."

"Like a dog."

"What's wrong with that?"

"Not a damn thing."

Anna reached out and took Mona's hand. "You know, when I come back, I want the bluebells to be in bloom."

Mona's heart swelled at the meaning of that. Not *if* but *when*. "I think that can be arranged," she said.

Far beneath them miniature versions of Michael and Wilfred appeared on the lawn. Michael yelled up to say that their taxi had arrived.

Mona cupped her hands around her mouth to shout her reply.

"Coming, Babycakes!"

They said their goodbyes in front of the house, while Colin's taxi idled nearby. A train station send-off would have been too momentous, Mona thought, as if it could be the last for all of them. It was best to keep it simple, here in the sunshine of Easley with Nilla's tail wagging them on their way. There was no promise of eternity, of course, but it was close enough for now.

Special thanks to . . .

Ian McKellen and Graham Norton for lodging me and Chris until we could find a home of our own here in London.

Lucinda Hawksley, whose book about Lizzie Siddal inspired me.

Roy Simpson and Sandy Ingram for their eagle-eyed early reading of this manuscript.

Michael Cashman and my solicitor, Barry O'Leary, who paved the way for our British citizenship.

My agent, Binky Urban, for overseeing my career with love and dedication.

My editor at HarperCollins, Millicent Bennett, whose belief in this novel kept me writing.

My friend and lecture agent Stephen Barclay, who fulfills my lifelong need to be on a stage.

My publisher Bill Scott Kerr at Transworld for repackaging all ten volumes of my Tales series and making me a Penguin at last.

My London literary agent, Gordon Wise.

My translation agent, Daisy Meyrick.

Allison Barrow, a brilliant publicist and longtime friend.

Jamie Neidpath, the 13th Earl of Wemyss and March, whose Stanway House has fed my imagination for forty years.

About the Author

A̲RMISTEAD M̲AUPIN is the author of *Tales of the City, More Tales of the City, Further Tales of the City, Babycakes, Significant Others, Sure of You, Maybe the Moon, The Night Listener, Michael Tolliver Lives, Mary Ann in Autumn, The Days of Anna Madrigal* and *Mona of the Manor*. He also wrote an acclaimed memoir, *Logical Family*. Three television miniseries starring Olympia Dukakis and Laura Linney were made from the first three *Tales* novels. *The Night Listener* became a feature film starring Robin Williams and Toni Collette. Maupin lives in London with his husband, Christopher Turner.